W9-CTO-526

## The critics on Jenny Siler

### ICED

'A terrific follow up to last year's *Easy Money*. She writes perceptively about outsiders at odds not only with the law, but with friends (a transvestite chum and a refugee lover), family (a mother who has scrambled her husband's brains with a bullet) and themselves. The world they inhabit is hostile, unsettling and intimately observed. There's little doubt that the author has seen it, been there, bought the T-shirt' *Literary Review*

'There are no easy answers in *Iced*, no convenient resolution . . . It's this unflinching honesty that sets *Iced* apart from its rivals. That and the dark, atmospheric quality of the writing' *Daily Express*

'Siler's second novel shows fine movement and rhythm. She handles the hard-boiled writing style with a natural grace, never sounding forced or stagy'

*Publishers Weekly*

### EASY MONEY

'Jenny Siler takes the reader for a seriously fast and scary ride in *Easy Money*. If you're like me, you'll end up checking your reading chair for a seatbelt!'

Ian Rankin

'A stunning crime debut' *Daily Telegraph*

'Once in a blue moon a new writer speaks up in a voice that gets your attention like a rifle shot. Jenny Siler has that kind of voice: clean, direct and a little dangerous'

*New York Times*

Jenny Siler is thirty years old. She grew up in Missoula, Montana. For much of her life she has travelled and worked her way around the world, starting as a prep-cook in the scullery of a men's soup kitchen, through working in a fish-cannery in Alaska pulling salmon roe, to being a nude sketch model at an art museum in Frankfurt. Her work, she says, has defined her and her writing.

*By Jenny Siler*

Easy Money
Iced

# ICED

JENNY SILER

ORION

An Orion paperback

First published in Great Britain in 2000
by Orion
This paperback edition published in 2001
by Orion Books Ltd,
Orion House, 5 Upper Saint Martin's Lane,
London, WC2H 9EA

A CIP catalogue record for this book is available
from the British Library.

ISBN 0 75284 359 1

Typeset at The Spartan Press Ltd,
Lymington, Hants

Printed in Great Britain
by Clays Ltd, St Ives plc

*For Keith*

# Acknowledgments

Thanks to the following people for their help along the way. Nat Sobel, my agent and so much more, for being constantly in my corner; I can't say enough to thank you. Jack Macrae, for knowing exactly what to say to get my best work out of me. My fabulous copy editor, Janet Baker, for working so hard to make me look good. Rachel Klauber-Speiden, for countless hours of careful reading. Linda 'Castro' Zimmerman and all the members of SEAL team Alpha at the MAC, for helping me stay sane. Meredith Norton, for her constant humor and camaraderie in crossing the Lac de Bordeaux. You're a better friend than I deserve. Undying gratitude as well to Daryl Gadbow, storyteller extraordinaire, for his fine piece of journalism on the Taurus Raging Bull.

Thanks as always to my family. To my father, John Siler, my grandmother Pat Siler, and Mike McCarthy. And of course to my mother, Jocelyn Siler, my number one fan. I love you so much. To Keith Dunlap, my dearest love and my best friend. I'm the luckiest person alive. And to Frank.

Special thanks to the entire community of Missoula, Montana, for all their support, and to Jim

Crumley and all the other extraordinary writers here, for welcoming me with such open arms. There's nowhere else I'd rather live.

# One

It was cold the night I went to pick up Clayton Bennett's Jeep, the tail end of the coldest day of the season so far. In Montana the calendar demarcation of winter from fall is nothing but a technicality. Up here, in the shadow of Canada, other people's idea of winter usually starts before Halloween, and this autumn had been no different: parka weather, thick frost on windshields, breath like gauze even in the afternoon sun. But not until the morning of December 20 did we feel the imminent promise of an animal frost and know that a deep heart of winter cold was screaming in from the north.

A cleansing wind had raked across the valley floor, and by morning the river was viscous with ice. Pushed down from Canada, the air reeked of the tundra, of glacier-churned dirt and stunted lichen. It was this smell that signaled that the first subzero snap of the season was on its way.

I had just gotten Bennett's file that afternoon, and from what little I'd read I'd figured on one of those rare easy-as-pie jobs. My boss, Flip, had given me a set of dealer's keys. All I had to do was get in the Cherokee and drive away. I'd planned on paying my visit sometime in the next couple of days, but when I heard on the radio about Bennett's death I thought I'd better head over to his office right away. There was no telling who else Bennett owed money to, and I wanted to be the first person there to collect.

Normally, it would have taken a while for news like this to hit the airwaves, but Bennett had been stabbed in a drunken brawl and the two Indians the cops suspected had disappeared. Local radio stations were broadcasting descriptions of the couple, urging everyone to be on the lookout. The place was crawling with cops when I pulled into the parking lot of the Super Six Motel, next to Bennett's office. I'd told myself to grab the Jeep and get out of there. I'm not too fond of anyone with a badge, and I had no intention of sticking around. But when I saw the scene unfolding in the river bottom, curiosity got the better of me.

I didn't know much about Bennett, only that he had run a charter business, a shifty little outfit called Big Sky Adventures that took tourists on backcountry flyovers and down to remote lakes for fishing. His office and makeshift apartment were in a shack on the northern bank of the Clark Fork, right across the river from the vacant tract of land where the old paper mill and tepee burners used to be.

It's a downtrodden section of town, a final vestige of the ugly industrial West that Missoula was still part of when I was a child. Before the yuppies from California arrived, cleaned up the waterfront, and passed laws that kept the mines upstream from dumping cyanide in the river. Before the quaint farmers' market and the latte bars and cafés selling veggie burgers and frozen yogurt moved in.

When I stepped out of my Ford truck onto the slick blacktop, the time/temperature sign at the casino across the street blinked, its lighted display changing from 16 to 18 degrees below zero. I took a breath and felt the tissue in my lungs freeze up. Behind the concrete hulk of the motel and Bennett's shack, the river bottom was lit like a movie set. A stand of leafless cottonwoods stood in stark relief, their trunks a pale and ghostly white. The river was close to frozen solid, and the milky crust of ice shone under the halogen glow of spotlights. In its center was a narrow rush of water, black and sinuous as an adder. This time of year the hours of darkness far outnumber those of daylight, and even when the sun is above the horizon it seems diminished. So there was something obscene about the brightness of the lights on the river and the naked trees.

They had pulled Clay Bennett's body from the weeds on the low-water island where he had been discovered and were carrying him toward us to shore. It took four men to hold the stretcher. They wore fishing waders under their ranch coats, and the rubber boots were plainly no good on the icy boulders of the riverbed. Even from up on the bank I could see their feet slipping, their shins ripping into the thin shell of the river ice.

When they reached the unfrozen channel, one of the men faltered, dipped his knee, and stuck his arm

3

out to keep his balance. The crowd in the parking lot let out a collective gasp. The stretcher tilted and Bennett's hand sprang up in a lazy wave, his flannel-shirted arm freed from the death grip of whatever had held it to his side. The expressions on the faces of the men carrying him changed suddenly. Terror overcame them, revulsion at the jerking movements of the dead, and they lost their grips.

The corpse's head and right shoulder lolled downward, as if he were contemplating a quick dip. One finger dangled in the current, then a whole arm, the side of his torso, a booted foot, until his entire body was immersed. It was incredibly graceful, the way he went in, his palm slightly upturned to the sky, the fingers loosely curled. And the movement of his body toward the water: like a leisurely dive on a hot day. It took them a few frantic minutes to fish him out, then another few to plod on through the river and up the crumbling bank.

Of all the things that happened, it's Bennett's body I will always remember. How he lay there sparkling and shimmering in the lights of the parking lot, a layer of ice encasing him. In the time it took to carry him from the river he had solidified. His arms were frozen to his sides, pinned where they belonged. The brittle skin around him looked like a thin cocoon. He was perfectly preserved, the violence of his death completely intact. His flannel shirt was torn, his chest mottled with pink rosettes, tiny bursts of blood, a dozen cuts around his heart. He was a large man, and suddenly his size struck me, his power, the thickness of his arms.

*

They hoisted him up into the ambulance and closed the double doors and then, because Flip has told me over and over how important time can be in cases like this, I walked across the parking lot of the Super Six toward the Big Sky Adventures office.

Bennett's brown Jeep Cherokee was parked just outside the front door. The dark windows of the office reflected the commotion at the motel, the rhythmic revolutions of a police cruiser's lights, the ambulance flashing red as it pulled onto Broadway. Out on the river, figures rushed in and out of the spotlights' glare. I heard a shout, then another, a cry of 'Rabbit!' from the brushy island. A shape burst onto the open ice, a man lumbering forward. Evidently it was one of the Indians they'd been looking for. He was making good time till he slipped and fell. In an instant a sea of uniforms was upon him.

Fishing in my pocket for the dealer's keys, I slid into the Cherokee like I belonged there. In the rearview mirror I could see them bringing the man up the bank, his arms twisted around his back, his wrists cuffed. He stumbled along, the weight of his chest slung forward. I shoved the key into the ignition, felt the engine cough to life, and touched my own wrist, thinking of the cold cuffs, the familiar sensation of the steel bracelets grating against my flesh. And I thought of the other Indian, the girl still out there, fugitive.

# Two

They say home is where the heart is, and maybe for some lucky people the saying holds true. For me, however, home was a place to come back to when there was nowhere else left to go. My last home was a cozy cell at a women's prison in New Mexico. I'm what you might call a petty criminal. Except for the one that finally sent me away, my offenses were small-time: bad checks, stolen merchandise, fraud. That's not to say I can't take care of myself if I have to. Like most anyone who grew up in Montana, I'm good with guns and I know how to fight.

I had the misfortune of getting caught on the one transgression that carried some weight – eighteen months' worth of weight, to be exact. When they released me last year, just before my twenty-ninth birthday, I was free and clear. No parole, no prospect of work, just enough cash for a bus ticket back to Montana. Missoula was never a happy place for me, but like I said, there was nowhere else left to go.

Besides, prison had given me plenty of time for introspection. At some point during my year and a half I had forged regrets about certain things.

Family, for instance, or the lack of it. In my lockdown dreams my mother opened her arms to me. My father and I walked together through sagebrush gray with autumn frost. I admit it, I came back looking for the same things most of us want: the benediction of forgiveness, some sense of kinship, people who might claim me as their own.

A respectable job was out of the question with a record like mine, but my new life plan was to play it straight for a while, so I began repossessing cars for GMAC. It seemed like a good compromise. I found a two-bedroom cottage in the block behind the Dairy Queen, just a five-minute walk from my old grade school. I rent from a little old lady who retired to Phoenix. It's a convenient arrangement. Mrs. Carter left me most of her furniture and housewares: fraying chairs with doilies pinned to the arms; pots and pans I rarely use; a heavy, scarred kitchen table. Our only communication is the check I send her each month. When I took the place, I didn't tell her about my job or my former residence. Those are the kind of details that can scare a potential landlady off.

She didn't seem to make a connection with my last name. Gardner has carried the reek of small-town scandal for about twenty years now, since my mother committed a transgression of her own. Though I suppose it's a common enough name that you wouldn't assume anything. Not to mention that two decades does a lot to dull the memory.

Until my enforced stay in New Mexico, I really never had a home. I left here when I was sixteen and lived wherever I could: bus stations, strangers' couches, city squats, and, later, out of the trunk of my car. I held no small amount of disdain for people with sofas and closets and lawn mowers. But I've joined their ranks now, and I'm beginning to see the appeal of having a home. I take a certain perverse pleasure in finding neighborhood council flyers tucked under my front door. When the PTA came around handing out McGruff Crime Dog posters, I took two, one for the front door and one for the back.

Missoula has always been the kind of town where neighbors wave and people stroll the streets on summer nights eating ice cream. This good cheer can bring a person down. Luckily there's enough sleaze under Missoula's veneer to make the place tolerable. The work I do helps out by keeping me in the circle of personal failure and despair. All in all, it's a good life and I can't complain. I've always been a stranger here, so it seems no different now, coming back to this place that has forgotten me.

I have met a man here, a refugee. I wouldn't call it love, the thing that exists between us. Desire, maybe, but not love. He has a way of putting the flat of his hand just beneath the back of my thigh so I can feel the electric bristle of the fine hairs there connecting with the skin of his palm. And sometimes, when we are in bed together, he will move my leg aside and press his mouth into the bald crease where my leg and pelvis connect, the place where you would open a bird to separate the darkest of the meat. When he does this I have to

8

grapple with my sanity. I have to hold on tight to my equilibrium.

It was after seven when I found the Cherokee's headlights and rolled forward, inching my way across the slick snowpack coating the parking lot of Big Sky Adventures. The onlookers were beginning to disperse, like roaches caught in the glare of a lightbulb: A few dark shapes scuttled behind the Super Six, heading for the broken-down trailers between the motel and the river.

It was too late to take the Jeep to the dealership, so I figured I'd park it at my house for the night. If I could track Darwin down, I could get a ride back to pick up my truck. I was just signaling to turn onto Broadway when a black sedan pulled in. It rolled past me, its rear end fishtailing dangerously close to the Jeep. I heard the squeal of brakes and the car reversed, backing up until the driver's door was even with the Cherokee's. The Jeep sat high, and the sedan's window was a good foot and a half lower than mine. I had to glance down to see the face on the other side of the glass. It was a Russian, a kid whose Camaro Darwin and I were supposed to have repoed a few months earlier. We never did take his car, but he looked like he still held a grudge. His mouth behind the window was round with surprise. He stared at me, jabbed his finger in the air, and pointed to the Jeep. I only saw him for a second; then the traffic thinned and I pulled onto Broadway and headed for Darwin's.

*

Darwin was already working for GMAC when I got hired on. It's an independent business, and she and I mostly work alone, but we help each other out when we can. It's easier to use a second driver for times like this, or when the tow truck is too conspicuous to use.

I don't know much about Darwin, only that she used to live down in Colorado. She was a junkie then, and when she gave up the smack and was looking for a fresh start, Flip offered her a job. Technically speaking, Darwin's a man. Her plumbing's still intact, and when she works the repos she dresses like a man, but she says she feels most natural in drag. The gender bending doesn't bother me. I haven't exactly led a sheltered life. When I was on the inside I knew all kinds.

Believe it or not, there's a bar in Missoula that features drag shows, attracting more talent than you'd imagine. Darwin had a show later that night, and when I pulled up in front of her house all the lights were on. I parked the Jeep and let myself into the living room.

'Darwin!' I yelled.

An old Diana Ross tape was blaring from the stereo, and I wasn't sure she heard me. I sat down on the couch and lit a cigarette. I could hear Darwin in the bedroom, her falsetto trying to keep up with the diva's. After a few minutes she came sauntering out, her hips swinging to the beat. She was wearing a gold spaghetti-strap dress and gold sandals with heels like weapons.

'What do you think?' she asked. She blinked her eyes theatrically, and her lids turned into two perfect crescents, bright green against her dark brown skin.

'Nice,' I said. 'New wig?'

She nodded and plumped the elaborate mass of blond curls shimmering at her shoulders.

'I got that Jeep Cherokee,' I told her, taking a drag off my cigarette, leaning forward toward an ashtray on the coffee table.

'No shit.' She crossed to the stereo and turned the volume down. 'You go over to Bennett's place?'

I nodded. 'Just came from there. My Ford's still at the Super Six. You follow me home with it, and I'll drop you at the Amvets.'

'Okay.' Darwin shrugged, fiddled with the hem of her dress. 'They catch those Indians yet?'

'Caught the man. I don't know about the girl. They were pulling Bennett out of the river when I was over there. Dropped him in the fucking water.'

'No shit,' Darwin repeated. She grabbed a pack of Virginia Slims up off the table and pulled one of the thin cigarettes out.

'Must've stabbed him a dozen times,' I remarked.

'Guess they were drunk, huh? It was still daylight when they hauled him out to the island. There's got to be a hundred windows look out on that part of the Clark Fork.'

'Got to be,' I said, looking up, taking in the bare expanse of her shoulders. 'C'mon. You better put a coat on, it's cold out there.'

Things had calmed down at the Super Six when Darwin and I pulled into the parking lot.

The hulking spotlights were still in place like sentinels along the bank, but they'd been turned off and the river bottom was inky black. I could hear the water when Darwin opened the door to get out, but I couldn't see it. Beyond the silvery trunks of the cottonwoods the darkness was impenetrable.

I watched Darwin climb into the cab of my Ford and eased the Cherokee onto Broadway for the second time that night. The wind had picked up, and loose snow from drifts edging the road danced across the asphalt. Across the street, Santa and his team of reindeer were perched atop the illuminated Safeway sign. A four-story-tall star of Bethlehem climbed the brick front wall of the Catholic hospital where they had taken Bennett.

I left the Jeep at my house, drove Darwin to the Amvets, and stopped off at Charlie's bar for a beer or two. It was a good crowd that night, faces familiar enough so I didn't feel like I was drinking alone but not so familiar that they seemed intrusive.

The TV was tuned to a cable news channel. Three talking heads glared out from the screen, their names beneath them in little red banners. They were part of the bored and wealthy horde who had declared themselves presidential candidates. With primary season mere weeks away the media had worked themselves into a frenzy. Because of the relentless coverage they'd been getting, the men's faces were as familiar to me as the red and white curves of a Coca-Cola can.

One of them was a conservative billionaire from

California. Harvey Eckers, the type on his banner read. No luck with a name like that, I thought, though he seemed popular enough. The second man was a movie star, a gray-haired actor who'd played the president so often he thought he could actually do the job. The last prospective candidate, Gregory Jacobs, was the most forgettable of the three, a solid career politician who seemed somewhat informed. I'm not usually very interested in politics, but the mudslinging of this campaign was proving entertaining. A week earlier Eckers had accused Jacobs of having a slumber party with some girl who worked in the Senate mail room.

'Turn that shit off,' a voice at the far end of the bar protested.

'Amen,' another customer agreed.

The bartender picked up the remote and flipped along till she hit an amateur boxing match, two scrawny Cuban kids with bright silk shorts hanging off their bony frames. One guy was clearly winning; the match had reached the sad and pathetic stage.

I was deep into a pint of Moose Drool and a basket of chicken wings when I glanced over and saw Amos Ortenson ambling past the pool tables, heading straight for me. Amos was tall and gangly, a kid still getting accustomed to his oversized body. His hair was shaved to fine stubble at the sides, molded into a spiky Mohawk on top. As usual, he looked like an extra from one of the Mad Max movies: combat boots and leather jacket, dog collar, steel spikes on his wrists and shoulders.

Post-apocalypse chic. He slid onto a stool next to mine, helped himself to my last untouched wing, and flashed me a rotten-toothed smile.

'How's my favorite repo lady today?' he asked.

'Fuck off, Amos,' I told him.

In a state that can lay claim to the Unabomber and the Freemen, Amos Ortenson stood out as a bona fide nutcase. When he wasn't out at the bars drinking and causing trouble, he washed dishes at a Mexican restaurant over on Broadway. But he was known for his television show. He had a weekly two-hour slot on the local public-access station.

The show had become quite a hit, more for its inadvertent comedic value than its content. Amos claimed to be an ordained minister, although from what I understood he'd bought his credentials out of the back of a tabloid newspaper. The show, called *Anarchy with Amos*, mostly consisted of Amos babbling about doomsday prophecies and government-sponsored mind-control projects. It was crazy stuff, and Amos had been known to go berserk on the set and smash things, but he was basically harmless. He was just a kid in need of some direction.

Undeterred by my less-than-friendly reception, Amos propped his elbows on the bar. 'You hear about those Indians?' he said, tearing at the sinewy chicken wing with his teeth. He'd just come in from outside, and the cold still clung to him. Smells of wood smoke and snow and a hint of sulfur emanated from the folds of his leather jacket. The mill must be running, I thought.

14

I took a pull off my beer and stood. 'I thought Charlie eighty-sixed you from here.'

Amos grinned, his mouth widening above his scraggly goatee. 'He said I could come back if I behaved myself.'

'Not very likely,' I mumbled, shrugging into my coat. With Amos for company I had no desire to stick around. I laid a couple of dollars on the bar for a tip. 'I'm outa here,' I told him. 'The rest of that pitcher's all yours.'

Amos's eyes ranged greedily toward the beer. He smiled, ignoring my goodbye. 'I saw them bringing him up from the river. Saw it out the window of my place.' Amos's place was a broken-down trailer that sat on blocks behind the Super Six. 'I heard she's Blackfeet, from up in Browning. Red Deer.' He bounced the palm of his hand against his mouth and whooped, like a kid imitating a war cry.

I was working the buttons on my coat but stopped short. 'What did you say her name was?'

'Red Deer,' he repeated.

I pulled my watch cap on, thinking about the name. Hell, I told myself, there's lots of Red Deers up there. It's like Jones or Brown.

'They're saying it was her stabbed him, not the man,' I heard Amos say as I turned to go. 'But I bet she ain't the one done it.'

'Why is that?'

He cocked his head and looked at me sideways, as if contemplating whether I was to be trusted or not. The anarchy symbol he had tattooed on his neck jumped in rhythm to his pulse. 'Just a thought,' he said slyly.

'Sure.' I looked back at him, trying to guess at the muddled thoughts that churned in his head. I could see the Roswell alien autopsy and the assassination of John F. Kennedy spinning against each other like clothes in a tumble dryer. 'Who was it this time, CIA? An army from the Golgon galaxy?'

Amos shrugged.

'See you later,' I said, and turned to go.

I let the Ford warm up and headed south through downtown, past the Oxford Saloon and the old Wilma movie theater. The Higgins Avenue bridge was slick and traffic crept along it, headlights tunneling into the darkness. Gusts of wind rocketed out of Hellgate Canyon, sent dervishes of snow leaping off the side of the bridge. A handful of huddled figures had stopped on the walkway and were staring out over the frozen river. I glanced down at the milky swath, then back in the direction of the old paper mill, Bennett's office, and the motel. And then I saw why the onlookers on the bridge had stopped.

Down on the ice a light flickered, then another and another, like stars or fireflies. Flashlights searching. Figures appeared along the northern bank, men in dark clothes, only their faces visible in the paltry light cast by the streetlamps lining the river.

So they've not found her yet, I thought, slowing the Ford, squinting to see. I whispered the name *Red Deer* to myself, murmured the words *good luck*. Not that the name mattered. Running was so familiar to me I would have wished luck to anyone in her shoes. The searchers' lights combed the far bank and disappeared beneath the bridge, heading downriver.

# Three

No one thinking in terms of pure habitability would put Montana very high on their list of places to call home. In winter, of course, there's the cold. Spring and fall, there's the cold as well. July races by, perfect, spectacular, the only livable month. In August the fires come.

Growing up, I loved the fire season, the perpetual dusk that hung over the valley, the extraterrestrial sunsets. At night orange flares dotted the mountains. During the day smokejumpers buzzed in and out of the airport, scarlet clouds of chemical retardant trailing their mammoth silver planes. Some afternoons, when lightning storms raked across the mountains, dozens of small fires smoldered in the thick cover of the evergreens.

If I think of my life in terms of combustion, it's this kind of lightning fire that comes to mind. Not a flash immolation but a slow kindling, a red ember smoking for hours, even days, until it explodes in the dry underbrush and the forest bursts into fiery tongues.

Though I can't pinpoint the instant when my life ignited, there are important moments I go back to again and again. Like the day almost twenty years ago when my mother shot my father. I was at a slumber party when it happened and didn't find out until the next morning, when our neighbor came to pick me up. She was not an unkind woman, but I have hated her ever since. I remember her face bobbing up the walkway of my friend Marianne's house, and the way she looked at me, a phony seriousness. And I remember her smile, peach lipstick, sweat shimmering on her upper lip: that last moment before my entire life shifted, hurtled around the bend and over the unseen cliff of disaster. Of course it's not her I hate, but the crassness of my own ignorance. There's a humiliation in the memory, in the night I passed without knowing, the idiocy of each movement. That awkward time between the calamity and my knowledge of it.

My mother's action was spontaneous, born of extreme anger, and she used the closest weapon at hand, an old Colt thirty-eight special my father kept in the drawer next to his side of the bed. My father was an avid grouse hunter, so things could have been worse. She might have found his twelve-gauge instead and transformed his head into a pulpy mush. But she didn't, and he got lucky and lived.

I say lucky, though I'm not certain he would agree. If he could still hold a conversation, I suppose we could ask him. The single bullet that my mother fired rocketed deep into the part of the brain that allows for complicated thoughts, effectively rendering my father a child. For my mother, it was a blessing, really. He is the perfect husband

19

now, mute and helpless and, as if that weren't enough good fortune, erotically incapable.

Of course, there were other moments when the dry kindling crackled to life. There were dark blooms of combustion long before the shooting, long after. Though I didn't know it at the time, the collision of Clayton Bennett's history and my own would prove to be one of those moments. Sometimes now the smell of winter air hits me, Christmas light, ice on the river, and I think of him, frost like dander in his hair. I think of Tina Red Deer and the Super Six Motel. A bright spray of blood on the walls. A battalion of police cars in the parking lot. Wet blue jeans iced to stiff boards. The hollow sound of a skull cracking against the boulders of the riverbed. All the unseen rudiments of tragedy.

When I got home I checked the Cherokee, making sure the doors were locked. I hadn't noticed it earlier, but there was a briefcase on the backseat. The case was metal, space-age in design, with round corners and a complicated combination lock, a cheap version of the kind of case a mad bomber in the movies might use. It was the only object in the otherwise neat Jeep, a relic of Bennett's life. Though I'm far from sentimental, I found it somehow poignant. And intriguing. I popped the door and leaned it on its side, imagining the Maltese Falcon, gold ingots, a cascade of South African diamonds.

'Schatze, no!' A piercing voice sounded behind me. Grabbing the case, I turned from the Jeep, let the door fall closed.

'No, Schatze! Come!' It was my neighbor, Mrs. Jenkins, a lumpy little woman with two fancy Siamese cats and a repulsive pug-nosed dog who likes to relieve himself in my yard. She was shapeless in a heavy coat, her gray hair pinned in curlers.

I looked down and saw the dog plowing through the snow. The animal stopped in front of me and barked several times, then clamped its teeth onto my pant leg, growling furiously.

'There, there,' Mrs. Jenkins said. She bent and gathered the dog in her arms, stroked the top of its head. Clucking her tongue, she flashed me a look of hatred, as if I had provoked the attack.

I watched her climb her front steps and then went inside, kicked my boots off, and shed my coat. Setting the case down on the kitchen table, I found a bottle of whiskey, cracked the top, and poured myself a hefty tumbler. Then I picked up the phone and dialed Flip's cell phone number.

My boss is an auditor for GMAC. For the most part, his job involves driving around the state and taking inventories at car lots. He checks up on sales figures and makes sure payments are getting made. He's a friendly man and a good talker, and generally, when people are falling behind in their payments, he's able to help them work out some kind of financial arrangement. It's only when diplomacy fails that Darwin and I enter the picture. Repossession, Flip has explained to us, is a last resort.

Flip knows about the stint I did in New Mexico, and though he's never mentioned it I'm fairly certain he knows about my parents. I'm grateful for the judgments he doesn't make, and for the job. It's one of the only legal occupations where my background comes in handy. The pay isn't great, but it's all in cash, and, like I said, Flip's easy to get along with. I do my job and he doesn't ask any questions.

'Watkins here,' he chirped, answering on the first ring.

'Hey, Flip. It's Megan.' I cradled the phone with my shoulder, pulled a cigarette from a pack on the counter, and lit it. 'Did you hear about Bennett?'

'Does a bear shit in the woods?' Flip is a walking Western cliché. This particular reply is one of his stock favorites. 'I guess this makes your job a whole hell of a lot easier,' he said merrily.

'Yeah. I picked up the Cherokee a couple of hours ago.'

Flip chuckled. 'Good going.'

'It was too late to take it to the lot, so I drove it over here. I can drop it off in the morning.'

'Whatever you say. I'm going to Butte on the twenty-third for Christmas with the wife's family. Just as long as I have it by then.'

'Sure thing.'

'Merry Christmas,' he said.

'Yeah, you too,' I told him.

Then I hung up and called Kristof.

Let's face it, all that time I spent on the road in my former life did little to ready me for the rigors of a kitchen. Anything harder than scrambled eggs or ramen noodles is a challenge for me. So when

Kristof knocked on my door at ten, I was just sitting down to a late dinner of microwave popcorn and Chicken and Stars soup. I'd been working at getting the case open, but it wasn't easy. I figured I'd try the hinges later since I wasn't having any luck with the locks.

'What is this?' Kristof asked, walking into the kitchen, pointing at the table with disgust.

'Something I found in the Jeep I repoed tonight.' I shrugged toward the case. 'Just curious.'

'No. What is this food?' he repeated.

'Dinner,' I explained, stuffing a handful of the popcorn into my mouth.

Kristof is Czech. He's been in this country fifteen years now, but he still struggles with the American concept of food.

'Please. We can go out. Whatever you want. You don't have to do this.' He said this seriously, as if he were a hostage negotiator and I was about to blow away another victim.

He removed the offending food from in front of me, opened the refrigerator, and searched the near-empty shelves. I lit a cigarette and watched him putter around the kitchen, opening and closing cupboards, rattling pans, manning the stove.

'You hear about that murder over by the river?' I asked.

Kristof nodded, distracted. 'I saw the news,' he said.

'You hear if they found that woman yet?' I took a drag off my cigarette, drew my heels up onto my chair.

Kristof nodded. 'I guess they caught up with her

somewhere near my place. Jacob's Island area.' He looked up at me and smiled, then turned back to his chopping and grating. I always think him beautiful when he cooks like this, the fine work his muscles do, his fingers light on the knife, his alchemic abilities. Through some miracle of faith he managed to cull together enough ingredients to make a meal. Pasta boiled in one pot and a thick, garlicky tomato sauce simmered in another.

He came over to the table and set two plates opposite each other, and suddenly I wanted to forgo the food and go straight to bed.

'They said she stabbed him,' he said, picking up the thread of our conversation.

I nodded, got up, and refilled my glass. 'Would you like a drink?' I asked.

Kristof set a knife down next to the plate that was to be mine, then a fork. 'I saw her picture on the television,' he said quietly. 'She was small, really. Her hands also. And so young. Not much older than we are.'

After dinner we lay on the living room floor drinking beer while we watched a cop show on TV. I brought the case out and fiddled with the lock for a while, then gave up and settled my head onto Kristof's chest. It was snowing on the screen, silvery-blue television flakes, thicker and wetter than the ones we get here in Montana. It was the dark end of the day in the picture, and somewhere in the distance a neon sign blinked off and on and off again. A man and a woman sat on wooden chairs in a small room with a window. As they talked, the TV snow kept falling, blanketing the city beyond the panes.

The man was tall and thin and dark. The woman was lovely. What they were doing was all about confession. For a while they fell silent. Then the woman turned her head so she could see the snow and said something. The man got up from his chair and put his hand under her hair, on the side of her neck. Now that she had told him, everything would be all right.

There was something about his hand, the way it rested there against her shoulder. Anyone watching this might have thought they were lovers. There was something about the snow, the slanted way it descended, its cold melancholy. It was as if they had just shed their clothes in that little room and made us witnesses to some great intimacy. It was almost pornographic.

Of course, they were not lovers. He was a cop and she was a whore. It was an old show, a rerun from a couple of years earlier, and I'd seen it before.

When the show was over Kristof clicked off the TV and we went into the bedroom. Outside, the snow lay like a cold pelt on the yard and the street beyond. Kristof took my face in his hands, and when I kissed him I could taste the alcohol in both our mouths, the sweetness of the malt. The hair at the base of his neck was damp and cool. The bedroom was chilly, and we stepped out of our clothes and slid in under the layers of flannel and down. His skin and hair smelled clean, like the purple throats of lilacs.

*

That night I dreamed about the Red Deer woman. I was back on the Higgins Avenue bridge with the lights of the searchers far below me. A lone figure ran in front of the crowd on the frozen river, a woman with long black hair. She was not dressed for the outdoors. Her bare arms pumped at her sides, working for speed. She looked back once, leapt across a soft spot in the ice, and skidded toward the riverbank, her breath rolling out in short hard bursts, her hands clawing at the powdery snow.

Several of the men stopped and raised their arms. The woman took a step upward and a gunshot sounded, echoing off the underside of the bridge like cold wood cracking. The snow next to her exploded. I watched her cringe and bring her hand up over her head. She glanced behind her, then recovered and moved on, finding her footing in the snow, scrambling easily up the bank now. The men started to run again, and a mass of cowboy hats and white faces converged beneath the woman. She looked back at them, leapt forward, crested the bank, and careened into the street, into the glare of my headlights.

I turned my head to hers, my eyes frozen on her face. She was younger than I had imagined, late twenties or early thirties. My age. Her cheeks were high and tight, bright pink from the cold. Her nostrils opened wide when she breathed, the way the wet nose of a deer will open, sucking at the air. Her skin was sensuous in its brownness, a color that elsewhere might suggest money and leisure, hours spent sunning on some warm palm-studded island. Here in Montana it's the color of poverty, of methadone clinics, sugary wine, and cheap houses painted the same shade of government green.

She looked at me hard, as someone would look at an enemy, or as an accuser might look at the accused. Not a look you would give a stranger. There was something unusual, even wrong, about her face, something that didn't quite fit. I studied the shape of her eyes, the nose, the way her chin jutted, looking for anything familiar, hoping I wouldn't find it. Then the first man came up, and the second, and in an instant she was pulled from my view.

My alarm clock read just past five when I woke to the sounds of shattering glass and a car door slamming. Muffled voices clamored on the street outside. Kristof slept soundly beside me. I crawled over him and walked to the bedroom window. I was the only person on my block to have neglected my holiday decorating duties. The whole street glittered gaudy as a fairground, with cascading icicles and three-dimensional Santas and reindeers.

In the glow from my neighbor's life-sized nativity scene I made out three figures loitering around the Jeep. One dangled a baseball bat from the crook of his arm and all three hopped back and forth, clapping their gloves together to stave off the cold. In their long black coats they looked like giant ravens in the snow. A fourth head bobbed inside the smashed driver's side window.

Turning to my closet, I fumbled along the dust-blanketed top shelf, feeling with my fingertips for

Mrs. Carter's old twenty-two revolver. I'm the first to admit it's not much of a gun. When I moved here, part of my new plan for a respectable life was to give up firearms. But this one came with the house. My landlady bequeathed it to me.

'You never know,' she had explained apologetically, looking out from under her puff of blue hair. 'You don't have to keep it, but I always liked having it around.' I couldn't have agreed with her more.

I mumbled a grateful prayer to her common sense as I lifted the gun from the shelf, found a pair of jeans on the floor, and stumbled into them. I grabbed a sweater off the doorknob and dressed myself as I made my way back through the living room and kitchen. My boots were by the back door, and I shoved my bare feet into them and stepped out into the yard.

My first sleep-riddled thought was that they were hotwiring the Cherokee. As I rounded the corner of the house I saw the beam of a flashlight dance across the backseat. One of the men said something and then they all laughed, but I was still too far away to make out what they were saying. It was mercilessly cold. Each breath I took froze the soft tissue in my lungs. I brought the gun up in front of my chest, cocked the hammer, and stepped out from behind the side of the house.

'Tell him to get the fuck out of the Jeep,' I said. 'Right now, out.'

The man with the baseball bat looked up and laughed dismissively. He slipped a pack of cigarettes from his coat and lit one.

I crossed the front yard and stepped through the snow, making my way toward the shattered window of the Jeep.

'Did you hear me?' I yelled, pivoting around, bringing my gun up level with the figure in the Cherokee.

It was the same bloated face I'd seen earlier, as I pulled out of the parking lot in front of Clay Bennett's office: Ivan Popov.

'Get out, now,' I told him.

'Put the gun down,' one of the men said, his voice flat with disdain and boredom.

I looked up and the man closest to me opened his coat, flashing me a view of a stubby short-barreled shotgun. He hoisted the weapon up, pointed it at my head, and racked the slide. The sound was loud in the frigid air.

Ivan flashed me a cruel smile. 'Looks like you're outnumbered,' he said, dropping the flashlight into his lap and reaching into his coat. He pulled out a black Ruger and set the tip of the barrel against my forehead.

The man with the baseball bat stepped toward me and lifted the twenty-two from my hand.

Ivan smirked. 'Next time, you might consider a real gun.'

He popped the Cherokee's door and got out, then nodded his head toward me and murmured something in Russian to the goon with the bat.

The man clamped his gloved hand into a tight fist and hit me square in the stomach. I doubled over, my breath knocked out of me.

'Where is it?' Ivan demanded.

'Where's what?' I wheezed.

'The case,' he said, pounding his right fist into the open palm of his left hand like a baseball player softening a glove.

I straightened myself and focused on Ivan's face, trying to wrap my tongue around the word. 'Inside.' His eyes were flat and black. Christmas lights winked in the irises.

Ivan nodded again and the goon's fist connected with my stomach a second time. Bile surged up sour in my chest. I spat into the snow, felt my shoulders jerked upward, my feet lifted from the ground. The Russians propelled me forward, around the side of the house, and in through the back door.

Ivan shoved me into a chair and grunted more directions in Russian. One of the goons headed through the kitchen and into the living room; he came back grinning, the metal case dangling from his meaty hand.

'Good,' Ivan said curtly. He motioned theatrically to me. 'Now, why don't we give the little woman her gun?'

I sat at the kitchen table and listened to the sound of their tires spinning in the loose snow, then fishtailing away from the curb and down the street. Fear and apprehension rose up bitter in the back of my throat. I kept remembering Ivan's expression when he saw me pulling onto Broadway in the Jeep, his finger punching the air. I ran through what little I knew about the Russian in my mind. He seemed like one of those small-time criminals with a dangerous yearning for the big leagues. Recently

I'd heard he'd been stealing cars, chopping them up for easy resale. Whatever he was doing, he was definitely bad news. It looked like Bennett had been involved, and coincidence or not he'd just gotten himself killed.

Footsteps shuffled across the living room carpet, and I looked up to see Kristof's face in the dark doorway.

'There was someone here?' he asked sleepily.

I put a cigarette to my lips. 'Some Russians,' I told him, striking a match, trying to hold my hands steady. My fingers wavered back and forth.

'Russians?' Kristof asked, stepping closer. He cupped his hands over mine to still them. The flame curled around the tip of the cigarette and the dry tobacco ignited.

'It's nothing important,' I lied, exhaling. The bare skin at my ankles was raw and itchy where snow had seeped in over the tops of my boots.

Kristof looked at me as if for the first time. I watched his gaze shift from my face to the kitchen table and the compact shape of the twenty-two.

'Nothing important,' he repeated, as if trying to convince himself.

He wasn't buying it. Neither was I.

# Four

Kristof went back to bed, but I was too anxious to sleep. I started a pot of coffee and stepped to the front window. The snow was a muddle of tracks: my boots emerging from the side of the house, crossing the yard, footprints where Ivan's thugs had stood, wheel tracks arcing away from the curb. Peering down the street, I saw the paper boy jogging along the sidewalk, his delivery bag bouncing against his hip. He paused at my walk and raised his hand, rocketing the paper straight to the front step.

I stepped onto the porch and ducked back inside, unrolling the cold paper. Violent crime is a rare occurrence in Missoula, and Bennett's murder made the front page. Amos had been right; the woman's name was Tina Red Deer. There was a picture of her being hustled through the doors of the jail. Framed by matted strings of dark hair, her face was tilted up to the camera, caught off guard. Her cheeks were dirty, smudged with sweat and blood. There was a dark bruise on the left side of her temple.

I took the paper into the kitchen, poured some coffee, and skimmed the article. She and the man,

Elton Williams, were both from Browning. According to the *Missoulian,* Tina and Elton met Bennett at the Trail's End, a bar and casino across the street from his office. The couple was staying at the Super Six Motel, and they invited Bennett back to their room for a drink. It was before noon when the bartender first noticed the threesome talking. It seemed evident Bennett hadn't met the couple before, though he was a regular at the Trail's End.

They left the bar all together around one, stopped at the convenience store down the road, and bought a sackful of forty-ouncers. Then they returned to Tina and Elton's room at the Super Six. Bill Jackson, the owner of the motel, saw them go up inside.

At around two-thirty in the afternoon, when the maid came to change the sheets in Room 1209, Tina and Elton and Bennett were watching *General Hospital.* They were loud and unruly, and they told the maid they were busy and she should skip the room.

Neither suspect could pinpoint how Clay had died, only that they had turned from the blurred images on the television and found him bleeding onto the mottled quilting of the bedspread. The couple remembered a discussion about going out for more malt liquor, but neither could recall if they had actually left. There was a gap in both their memories here, a mutual loss of consciousness that began with a commercial for denture adhesive and ended with a moment of confusion, brought on by the inconsistency of the alert openness of Clay's eyes and the stiff blade plunged deep into his rib cage.

At three-forty-five, Tina knocked on the door of the adjacent room. The front of her shirt was bloodstained, and an unlit cigarette was in her right hand.

'Hey, mister,' she said to the occupant of Room 1210, 'you got a light?'

She balanced herself on the doorjamb, leaving claret palm prints smeared along the white wood, while the man ducked back inside to find some spare matches.

'I found her a whole pack,' he explained in the paper. 'I sure as hell didn't want her coming back.'

And then, for reasons only Tina and Elton could understand, the couple decided to take the dead man out across the river and bury him there, in broad daylight, on the low-water island in the center of town.

I put the paper down. Tina Red Deer stared out at me, her face the face of a half-breed.

Snapshot of my parents. It's the Fourth of July, the summer before I enter the fourth grade. We're up at Flathead Lake, anchored off Finley Point. This is the reservation, and everything explosive is legal. Though it's still mid-afternoon, smoke trails flare up from the beach: bottle rockets, artillery shells. Firecrackers rattle like machine-gun fire, a preview of what's to come.

My parents' friends, the Torvalds, have come up for the long weekend. Both couples are elegant and young, the women sleek in their bathing suits. But there is something spectacular about my parents, something sexy. There's a practiced ease to the way they do things, as if they'd been born wealthy. Watching them, you would never guess they were both the children of Havre wheat farmers. My mother's hair is lush and red, tied loosely above her neck. When my father dives from the bow of the boat, his body makes a perfect arc.

My mother and Mrs. Torvald make margaritas in the cabin while the men talk about work. They are both lawyers at the same firm, though they have different specialties. My father is an expert in questions of land use, water and mineral rights mostly. He counsels for the tribes and makes good money, enough to buy this boat, our house on Rattlesnake Creek, the cabin with its porch that overlooks the lake.

I'm in the water when the patrol boat approaches, and my mother waves me back on board. She throws a kimono over her suit and the five of us stand on deck and watch the little craft grow closer. The man driving is an Indian, close to my father's age, with two long braids. He smiles at me when he pulls up beside us, as if he and I were sharing a private joke. He asks to count our life jackets and then stands there watching while my father scrambles belowdecks. He has on cowboy boots, a brown uniform, and a badge that says TRIBAL POLICE.

My mother lights a cigarette and taps her fingernails nervously on the side of her margarita glass. When my father comes back short one life jacket she rolls her eyes, pulling her robe tight around her. My father is sorry, but the Indian smiles and writes him a ticket anyway. 'Happy Fourth,' he says when

35

he leaves, tipping his hat toward me. And I know from the way my mother breathes, the way she flicks her ash across the clean white deck, that she is not happy.

'Harassment,' she says, when the man is gone. 'They only ticket whites.'

'It's a stupid law,' Mrs. Torvald agrees feebly.

My mother is not appeased. She looks at my father as if this was all his fault. 'You'd think you might get some consideration,' she sneers. 'You're practically a member of the tribe.'

I am nine years old, puzzled by my mother's suggestion. It's not until much later, when I enter the adult world of sexual banter, that I will realize what she means by this, that it has something to do with my father's preferences. But even at nine I understand that this remark has nothing to do with the work he does. And I understand that my father is allowed to say nothing in his own defense. He has to stand there and take it like he always does.

I wasn't eager to take the Cherokee to Flip. The broken window looked bad in the pallid light of morning, and there was a long gash in the brown finish. My guess was that the Russians had taken a crowbar to the metal. Kristof left for work around nine, and I headed out of town in my truck. I had a repo up in Superior to check on, which was as good an excuse as any for killing time.

It was a slow drive up the river. The highway wound into slick corners through the cold shadows of the Bitterroot Range and the Nine Mile Divide.

Bare patches of stubble left by recent logging were highlighted by new snow. Outside of Alberton the Missoula radio stations faded to dead static.

With only the dull whir of the truck's heater to distract me, my mind turned to Tina Red Deer, stuck on her like a needle against worn vinyl. I pictured Clayton Bennett's arms, the muscles taut, still remarkably powerful for someone his age. The file I'd gotten from GMAC said he was sixty-five. They said she had stabbed him. But somehow I couldn't quite imagine how she might have accomplished this, drunk as she must have been. Thin as her cold frame had looked.

They were nasty thoughts, fraught with trouble, none of my business. I tried fruitlessly to push them out of my mind. But there was something persistent about Tina, the bad coincidence of the name, the two words like the sulfured tip of a match drawn across a grainy flint. It made me think of the world of my father's transgressions, appetites he still paid for.

Superior was a bust. The owners of the car I was looking to nab had evidently packed up and left town in a hurry. The house they'd been renting was dark and empty, the floor strewn with small things they'd dropped or forgotten in their haste: a single pink sock, a ski hat with rainbow stripes. I stopped at the gas station on the way back to Missoula, filled the truck up, and bought a box of coconut snowballs, some coffee, and a fresh pack of cigarettes.

It was still early when I got home, just past

lunchtime. Even with the sugar and nicotine fueling my body, I could feel the previous night's lack of sleep catching up with me as I climbed out of the Ford and headed up my porch steps. The postman had come, and my box was stuffed with the usual junk: bills, holiday flyers, coupon books. I tucked the mail under my arm, put the key in the lock, and opened the front door.

There's a specific kind of anger that comes with the knowledge that someone has been in your home. Breaking and entering is a terrible thing, a violation. Even when I was desperate for money, it wasn't something I did. So when I stepped into my living room my first sensations were ones of rage. The house had been ransacked. Books were strewn around, pages ripped from their covers. The cushions had been torn off the couch, the fabric shredded.

'Jesus,' I said to myself, dropping the mail, reaching my hand back to close the door. A jolt of fear pulsed along my spine.

'Don't move,' a voice whispered from behind me. I felt a hand on my shoulder, then a pain on the side of my neck, sharp and intense as a bee sting. 'Don't move or I'll cut you.'

I shifted my eyes carefully downward, saw gloved fingers, the blunt handle of a knife.

'Where is it?' my assailant asked. It was a woman, her voice low and smoky. I could feel her chest on my back, the thickness and power of her body. She felt large, not fat but muscular, bigger than I was by quite a bit.

'Where's what?' The words were ominously

familiar, a repeat of last night's conversation with Ivan.

She jabbed the knife deeper and I winced at the pain. I could feel a warm trickle of blood on my neck. 'That case,' she hissed. 'The one you took from the asshole's Jeep.'

'I don't have it,' I told her, my stomach reeling, nauseated.

'I don't care.' I felt the blade of her knife slice across my neck. It was a shallow incision, meant as a warning. 'Find it,' she said, releasing my shoulder. 'I'll be back.' Then she opened the door and was gone.

The cut was clean and straight as a surgeon's. By the time I stumbled to the bathroom mirror the skin had closed onto itself. Tiny beads of blood welled along the laceration like jewels on a dainty choker. I sat down on the edge of the tub, pressed my right cheek up against the cool tiles of the shower, and relived the solidity of the woman's chest on my back.

'Find it,' I heard her say. She'd scared me, and I don't scare easily. I leaned forward, rested my head in my palms, and felt my heart hammering in my chest.

Clayton Bennett was dead, I told myself, and more than one person was looking for what he'd left behind. I closed my eyes and pictured his body, the cuts dark as the bruised petals of a rose, his skin blue like snow in the diffuse light of dusk. Ivan Popov had come and now this woman, wanting something I didn't have. She'd put a knife to my throat and I needed to know why, needed to be ready when she came back a second time.

My legs were still weak when I stood up. I washed my face, combed my hair out, and tucked it up into a tight bun. By midafternoon I had the truck warmed up and was heading west along the interstate.

# Five

Technically speaking, the Russians in Missoula are not Russian. They're mostly from smaller countries that were once part of the Soviet Union: Belarus, for instance, or Ukraine. But in a nation weaned on duck-and-cover films, the Cold War dies hard. For most of us, the complex web of Soviet imperialism is far too difficult to decipher. So, Russian or not, that is how these newcomers are known.

The first wave of immigrants to find their way here from the motherland were the Christians. Theirs was a dream of middle-class America, of shopping malls and water parks and Jerry Falwell's face beaming into the bowls of their satellite TVs. I see them now and then at the video stores and the supermarkets, haggard women who look twenty years older than they are, with packs of six or seven children in tow.

The second wave of Russians were looking for a different kind of prosperity. Raised on bootlegged videos of *Rambo, The Godfather,* and *High Noon,* they looked toward the West and envisioned a land where guns were easy to come by, law enforcement was of the Barney Fife variety, and *taxes* was a dirty word. Ivan Popov's father, Nick, was one of the first to ride this second wave.

Nick's a criminal of the old-school variety, the Don Corleone of western Montana. Classy and discreet, he only deals with high-ticket ventures. I met him last summer when Darwin and I were sent to repo Ivan's Camaro. Nick was waiting for us outside his son's apartment when we came for the car, and he had a proposal for us.

He took us inside and handed us each a stack of crisp bills.

'Please. If you could tell your boss you have been unable to locate the automobile, I would be in your debt.' He spread his arms in a theatrical gesture of common trust. 'My son is most irresponsible. I am certain we can work something out.'

We agreed, and a week later Flip called. 'What do you know?' he said. 'That Russkie with the Camaro came through on his payments. Brought the rest of what he owed on the car into the dealership in cash. I think we'll let him keep it.'

It's nice to be owed – even nicer if the time comes when you need a favor, and you know you can collect.

The Popov place is up in Hot Springs, a town north of Missoula on the far western side of the Flathead Indian Reservation. Calling Hot Springs out-of-the-way is an understatement. The town sits at the end of a road that goes nowhere, and in Montana *nowhere* tends to live up to its name. There are hot springs in Hot Springs, and at the turn of the century some well-meaning investors built a bathhouse there and a luxury hotel. Though by no means luxurious, the hotel is still there, but the bathhouse has long since fallen into ruin. All that remains of the project is a crumbling smokestack and two murky cement-bottomed hot pools.

The turnoff to Hot Springs from Highway 93 is in Ravalli. When I got there a squall was blowing down off Evaro Hill and driving was bad. I turned into the parking lot of the Bison Café and went inside for some coffee while I waited for the weather to clear. It was closing in on five o'clock before the gravel trucks came through and I could start again. The sky was black and blue, punched by a sickle of moon.

Even in the wake of the sander it was hairy driving, and I was grateful for having turned my hubs to four-wheel drive. Skirting the Flathead River, I headed west to Perma, then north across the river. After Perma the road flattened out into Camas Prairie, a wind-scoured bowl said to be the roaming place for all the Flathead ghosts. There were no spirits visible that night, just a thick fog that coated the valley floor and a herd of white cattle whose eyes caught the glare of my headlights.

By six I'd crested the hill out of Camas and was heading down into Hot Springs. Signs for various businesses lined the road. MAGIC WATERS SPA, one said, rushing into the beam of my headlights. Another announced the HOT SPRINGS HOLISTIC HEALTH CENTER. I've made countless trips up here, and I have yet to find ninety percent of these establishments.

Entering the city limits, I slowed the truck and cruised through downtown, past the town's three major businesses: the Cowboy Bar, the Pioneer Bar, and the Montana Bar. Popov's house, or, as the locals are fond of calling it, the Hot Springs dacha, sits on top of a hill overlooking town. The structure was originally an evangelical church, but the believers moved out years ago. Because Popov never bothered to take the cross off the roof, the place was easy to find even in the dark. I pulled the Ford up in front, climbed out, and walked up the steps. It was Nick who answered the door. He was in a white terry bathrobe, a cigar clamped firmly between his lips. Though it had been months since we met, he recognized me immediately and ushered me inside.

'Ah,' he said, leading me through the foyer and into the pool area, 'the young lady who was so discreet in the matter of my son.'

The inside of the old church was long and wide. Popov had taken the pews out and sunk a lap pool into the hall of worship. Rhomboid reflections quivered off the water's aquamarine surface, danced across the vaulted curve of the ceiling. There was a persistent echoing drip in the room. And from somewhere in the bowels of the building I could hear the tinny four-four strains of disco music.

Popov sank into a wicker couch and motioned for me to join him. 'May I offer you something? Some dinner, perhaps? A drink?'

'No, thank you.' I shook my head.

'Tea, at least,' he insisted. 'You must allow me to

44

be a good host. The waters here are very therapeutic.' He plucked the cigar from his mouth and beamed at me. There was a ministerial quality to him, an edge of forced cordialness. The same slightly uneasy feeling you might get from a good con man.

'Sure,' I said. 'Tea.'

Twisting his head over his shoulder, Popov bellowed commandingly toward a dark doorway at the back of the empty hall. 'Vera, *chai*,' he boomed. He clapped his hands several times and turned back to me, still smiling.

'So how can I be of help?' There was just the smallest hint of an accent to his voice, deep and villainous, like the accents of Russians in Cold War movies. 'I assume that is why you are here. At this hour.'

'I need some information,' I began, but before I could finish, a figure appeared in the doorway.

It was a woman. Her dark hair was teased into a high mass of curls, and she was wearing a skimpy spandex aerobics outfit. She took a step into the pool room and screamed something in Russian. From her tone and the way she flung her arms wildly, I guessed it was a long string of obscenities, evidently directed at Popov.

He kept his back to her while she yelled, breaking his benevolent smile only once, to take a long pull off his cigar. When she was finished she disappeared back through the doorway.

'My lovely bride,' Popov calmly explained when she had gone. 'She will bring us some tea. Please, go on.' He adjusted the corner of his robe, pulling it

45

down over his exposed knee. The smell of the cigar mingled unpleasantly with the sharp odor of chlorine.

'There was a theft last night,' I said, carefully measuring his response, hoping to get a feel for how much he knew about what his son was up to. 'From my home.'

Popov didn't flinch. 'Something of value was taken?'

I leaned forward and rested my elbows on my knees, trying to create an aura of criminal confidentiality. 'That's the problem, Nick. I don't know.'

Popov rested his cigar delicately against the side of a cut-glass ashtray. He curled the fingers of his right hand in toward his palm and examined his nails. 'It is a shame.' He sighed. 'But, like you, I am ignorant in this matter.'

'I was hoping to talk to your son about it, hoping you might know where to find him. I've heard he's got a chop shop out in East Missoula.'

Nick nodded. 'The boy is a menace. Too much American television, you know. But what can you do? I told him stealing cars is for – how do you say?' He searched for the right word. 'Hoodlums.' Stopping himself, he looked over at me. 'I meant no offense, Miss . . .'

'Gardner,' I said, helping him out. 'None taken.'

Popov's wife came back into the pool room carrying a black lacquered tray with a pot and two cups. She was silent this time, and I watched her walk the length of the pool in brand-new Nikes. She looked to be in her forties, attractive in that former-beauty-queen way. Her face was hard and seasoned, her skin caked with too much makeup. Unfolding the tray's legs, she set the tea in front of us and hissed something in Russian. I couldn't understand the words, but the tone was unmistakable. Her voice was mocking and mean, in the way only the voices of aging pretty women can be. As if the humiliation of others can keep their own mortality at bay.

'Vera.' He sighed, fingering the end of his cigar, turning slightly to watch her walk away. 'Do you know what *Vera* means?'

I shook my head.

'In Russian it means faithful. But I am too old for her. I should have known better. She hates me.' Reaching forward, he poured a stream of tea into one of the cups. He spooned a dollop of raspberry jam into the hot liquid, handed it to me, and then fixed a cup for himself.

'You know the old Texaco on Highway 200?' he asked suddenly, as if he'd been pondering what to tell me and had just now come to a decision. 'That's Ivan's place.'

I nodded. Beyond Nick, at the far end of the hall, I could see remnants of the old altar, rectangular marks in the paint where it had been ripped from its place on the wall. The floor around the pool was done up in white tile. Potted palms stood in the four corners of the large room like sentries. No doubt Popov had spent plenty on the place, but there was an element of shabbiness to it. Black veins of mildew had crept into the grout around the pool. Brown water stains mottled the high ceiling like sweat rings on an old pillow. It was a ruin of a ruin.

'One more thing,' I said, taking a chance. 'Do you happen to know if your son had business dealings with a man named Clayton Bennett?'

Popov closed his eyes and took a long pull on the cigar. His lids were heavy, gates meant to contain or defend. I could hear the dry tobacco crackling as it burned. 'I'm sorry I could not be of more help,' he said finally, ignoring my question.

I took a sip of my tea, then put the cup down and got up. 'You might tell him,' I said, 'if you see him: There's someone else looking for whatever it is he's taken. She paid me a visit this afternoon. Didn't seem real happy about the situation.'

I headed back the way I'd come, up over the high saddle and down into Camas Prairie. The wind had kicked up full force by the time I passed the old Camas schoolhouse, choking the highway with drifted snow. I turned the radio on and got nothing but bad Christmas music and the Christian station.

On the far side of the Perma bridge I pulled the truck over and let the engine idle. A car whipped by, heading south toward Dixon and Ravalli. The road to the north was quiet. Too deep and fast at this stretch for freezing, the river was speckled with fat slabs of ice. I cracked the window and lit a cigarette, watching the reflection of the coal flaring in the windshield, the outline of my mouth visible when I inhaled.

The skin on my neck was tight where the wound had started to heal and I brushed away the meager

48

crust of blood, my mind flashing involuntarily to the woman in my house. If I could have stepped back through the last twenty-four hours, to the parking lot of the Super Six, I would have hesitated a few moments longer and let Ivan take the Jeep. Bennett didn't concern me. Neither did whatever was in the case. I wished I had kept it that way, but it was too late. The mystery now was how I planned to dig myself out of the dangerous hole I'd stumbled into.

A great chunk of ice floated out from under the bridge and caught on a driftwood snag. The river broke around it, churning like frothed milk, the true strength of the current revealed.

There was another puzzle forming in the back of my mind, caught among the questions of self-preservation like a fly in clean white paint. It had to do with Tina Red Deer, with the moment of erasure in which Bennett was killed. Suddenly I thought about the dark place where she was going, the doors slamming shut behind her, the locks clicking into place.

Another car appeared out of the darkness. Two bright headlights curved around the bend and blinked to red as they receded into the woods. I shifted into drive and rolled forward, my wheels turning slowly to the north. Away from Missoula and up toward the dark labyrinth of the Buffalo Bill Divide.

# Six

Just this side of Paradise. That's what my mother has always told people when they ask where she lives. She laughs when she says it, chuckling in that bland washed-out way she has taught herself. It's a bad joke, getting worse with wear, but it's true. My mother's place sits back in the woods, a couple of miles southeast of Paradise, Montana.

We lived in Missoula when I was a kid, in a beautiful stone house on Rattlesnake Creek with tall windows and a garden where my parents entertained. The shooting changed all that. There were medical bills, legal bills. In one year, with no money coming in and no prospect of any in the near future, we went from upper-middle-class to dirt-poor. But it wasn't just our income that changed.

There was little question that my mother would get off. There's a common saying in Montana that in this state everyone is entitled to one spouse. The justice system here still clings firmly to its Old West roots, and cheating husbands and wives tradition-ally get very little sympathy from a jury. It may seem hard for outsiders to believe, but the simple truth is that, although you can still serve time for running over a neighbor's cow, crimes of passion usually go unpunished.

My mother's case never even made it to trial. She claimed self-defense, saying my father had come home late and drunk and in the darkness she'd mistaken him for an intruder. There was a young detective on the case, a man who stood in the foyer of our house with his hat in his hand and blushed when my mother spoke to him. She was beautiful, I'm sure, tall and elegant, her eyes still red from crying. Even then I knew her allure was not in her looks but in her weakness, her vulnerability. The young cop didn't stand a chance. In the end he wrote it off as an accidental shooting.

Most everyone knew what had really happened that night, knew my father had come home reeking not of liquor but of another woman. My mother may have gone free, but she didn't go unpunished. Her actions and my father's were scandalous trailer-park behavior, not the conduct of a lawyer and his beautiful wife. There were no more garden parties for my mother. No more afternoons on the lake. No Christmas teas. She sold the cabin and the boat. Four years after the shooting, she sold the stone house and bought a small chunk of land by Paradise and a mobile home to go on it. Two years later I decided to leave.

She and my father live together still, a blissful couple. The transformation my mother has undergone is so complete that she no longer bears any resemblance to the person who raised me. She wears flower print dresses with high necks and choking ruffles. She makes banana bread and tapioca pudding for my father. In her kitchen are framed sayings she has stitched in needlepoint. SMILE, GOD LOVES YOU. THE LORD IS MY SHEPHERD.

When the ladies from her church come over to pray with her, they cluck their tongues and shake their heads while my father drools into his Cream of Wheat. She is a saint, they say. Just look how she takes care of him. All these years. Such love.

But I know the caretaking is my mother's greatest act of cruelty. Sometimes I imagine them alone in the tiny trailer. I imagine unspeakable acts, humiliations. I see my mother coming naked to his bed at night, her red hair brushing across her breasts. A mockery. A glimpse of what he can never again have.

It was still early when I pulled up in front of my parents' place. The wind had grown fiercer. It whistled across the side of the trailer, battering the dejected plastic wreath that hung from the screen door. I knocked hard and watched my mother's face appear behind the glass. She scowled, apparently annoyed by my unexpected presence. As if I'd interrupted an important needlepoint project or *The 700 Club*.

I can count the times I've spoken to my mother in the last fourteen years on two hands, maybe one. When I came back from New Mexico I imagined some kind of reconciliation. Though I realized we would never be the Cleavers, or even the Bundys, I thought we might at least salvage the years that remained.

The week after I got back to Missoula I drove up here. It was early fall, a chilly night. I stopped my truck at the turnoff to the driveway and watched them inside the lighted windows of the trailer. I could see my father in front of the television, his head limp on his neck. My mother got up occasionally, bustling from the living room to the kitchenette and back. I wanted to go inside more than anything, wanted to open the door of the truck and step out onto the gravel road, but somehow I couldn't bring myself to do it. Finally, my mother turned off the TV and the lights, and I left.

I came up the next month, and a couple of months later, maybe half a dozen times in all since I'd been back. I can't say what kept me from knocking each time. Anger. Fear. Things I can't understand, can't begin to name.

I looked at my mother in the doorway now, counted back to the last time we had stood face-to-face: four years, maybe five.

'Come in,' she said stiffly, as if I had been there only last week.

I stepped inside, taking in the shabby interior: yellow shag carpet, pink floral couch, plastic Christmas tree, a painting of a beatific Jesus, soft rays of light streaming from his head. Everything worn but clean. Layers of cooking odors clung to the curtains. An old Lawrence Welk Christmas special flickered on the television. A troupe of busty blondes in elf suits danced across the screen.

'Your father's in bed,' my mother volunteered.

She walked into the kitchenette and returned with a plate of cookies, little trees coated in green sugar. 'I heard you were back in Missoula.' She set the cookies on the coffee table.

'How's Pop?' I asked, perching myself on the arm of a La-Z-Boy.

'Same as always.' She sighed. 'How long have you been back?'

'A little over a year.' I started to tell her about New Mexico but stopped myself. The revelation seemed too generous in its intimacy.

'Would you like something else?' she asked, smiling, motioning to the cookies. Behind her was a poster: a poem and a picture of footprints on a sandy beach. I read the last line of the poem: *It was then that I carried you.*

'That Red Deer woman, the one Pop knew up on the Blackfeet Reservation, what was her name?' This was the question I had come to ask.

My mother flinched, her fist tightening around the hem of her housedress. For an instant I could see a shadow of her former self, an animal struggling within her. She picked up one of the cookies and bit it in half, feigning distraction. 'Hmmm?'

'Red Deer,' I repeated. 'She did some work for Pop when he was up in Browning.'

'I don't know, Meg. That was so long ago.' Her composure was fully restored. She glanced at the television, the floor, her eyes trying to avoid me. The elf women sang cheerfully, their Christmas medley punctuating the thick silence.

'There was a girl,' I said. 'About my age.'

My mother put her hands in her pockets, took them out again, looked at me blankly.

'The Red Deer woman,' I repeated. 'She had a child. What were their names?'

She shook her head slowly, held the plate of cookies out to me. The trees were perfectly shaped, each one an exact replica of the others. Her right knee was shaking. 'Sorry,' she said.

I nodded. *Sorry*. The first two buttons of her dress were undone, and when she leaned forward the tops of her breasts tightened against the fabric. For an instant I saw myself as part of her, and her as part of me. I saw my spine curled against the back of her womb, my hands waving like gills at my cheeks, her heart beating above my head. Here she was, this person in whom I had lain, of whom I had eaten.

I stood and started for the closed bedroom door.

'He's asleep,' my mother hissed, setting the plate down with a thump. Her voice was panicky, possessive.

I pushed the door open, stuck my head into the bedroom. My father lay on his side, snoring quietly. The air smelled of talcum powder, bodily fluids. The odor of a baby or an invalid. I pulled the door shut, turned back to my mother.

'I wish I could ask you to stay,' she said, fiddling nervously with her dress, giving no explanation as to why I had to leave.

She got up and walked to the door, put her hand on the knob.

'Maybe you could come and visit some other time. I know he would like it.'

'Sure,' I said, bracing my body for the cold. 'Merry Christmas.'

It was pushing midnight when I got back to Missoula, and food and sleep were the only things on my mind. I picked my way through the ransacked chaos of the living room toward the kitchen. My answering machine was blinking. I hit the playback button, poured myself a tumbler of bourbon, opened my cupboard, and scanned the contents. The first message was from my neighbor, Mrs. Jenkins. She was babbling on about the previous night, about how this is a quiet neighborhood and in the future could my friends and I please keep it down. She went on to remind me that the wind had drifted snow from my yard and I needed to shovel the walk out front. The second message was from Kristof, asking me to please call him when I got in.

The first time I met Kristof was last spring at the Union Club. He and some of the guys from his work are in a blues band, Homesick Eddy, and they play there some weekends. I was on a job, looking to nab the drummer's Cutlass Sierra. On their break between sets, Kristof came and sat at the bar next to me.

'Are you Eddy?' I asked him.

'No. There is no Eddy,' he explained. That was all we said to each other.

About a month later I ran into him at Bernice's Bakery. He was sitting outside with his coffee, feeding the remains of a muffin to a group of sparrows that had congregated on the sidewalk. I sat down a few feet away from him and started reading my paper. It was early and still quiet. The birds' beaks made a barely audible tapping sound on the sidewalk. Kristof's fingers rustled against each other. And he spoke to them in his language, in what sounded more like a song than speech. I listened for a while, then put my paper down and looked at him.

He was intent on what he was doing, and unusually beautiful, caught in this instant of concentration. I imagined him old, in some other city perhaps, his arms stretched out as they were now. And then he looked up, saw me watching, and straightened himself, suddenly self-conscious.

'I know you,' he said, scanning my face, trying to place me. The sparrows jumped at the sound of his speaking voice, scattered.

A few days later we bumped into each other at the grocery store. My basket was stacked with frozen dinners: rock-hard turkey tetrazzini, tuna casserole, meat-loaf dinner with apple crisp for dessert. Kristof looked at me in horror. His own cart brimmed with what, to me, seemed like exotica: green vegetables, fresh fruit, butter, flour, dark olive oil, massive heads of garlic.

'Are you following me?' I joked, laughing.

'No, of course not.' And he disappeared down the canned food aisle.

Later, as I was getting into my truck, he came up to me in the parking lot.

'Could I make dinner for you sometime?' he asked.

'Sure.' I shrugged.

'Tonight?' There was an urgency to his voice, as if I desperately needed his help but didn't know it.

'Okay,' I agreed. 'How about a picnic?'

We went to the drive-in. They were showing one of those asteroid movies that have been so popular lately. Kristof brought a cooler full of food I could never have imagined: tiny pies stuffed with vegetables and fresh herbs, trout smoked over cherry wood, sweet pickles, miniature huckleberry tarts. We sat in the bed of my truck under heavy blankets and gorged ourselves while New York and Paris were reduced to rubble. Moths shone like falling stars in the light from the projector, and the paper mill, just two fields away, spewed plumes of steam and smoke into the cloudless sky. It was the beginning of a long stretch of perfect summer nights that lasted all through July and August.

After the movie we went back to my house and lay in the grass looking up at the dark canopy of the maples. The air coming off the mountains was cold, the yard dense with the smell of Mrs. Carter's honeysuckle and her pollen-heavy lilies. For a brief moment I was reminded of a stint of mine down in Miami, of the frangipani and the mock orange bushes in the back garden of our apartment in South Beach, of the lushness of the tropics, the way the air seemed thick like a liquid. I could feel Kristof beside me, his bare arms stippled with goose bumps. He sat up and leaned over me, and his throat was pale and exposed in the light from the house.

'How old were you when you came to this country?' I asked.

'Eighteen,' he said, putting his hand under my shirt, resting his knuckles in the bowl of my stomach.

'Have you been back?'

He shook his head. 'After I left, they took my mother's job away. She was an architect, and she had to go clean the washrooms in the train station in Prague.'

He leaned forward as if he was going to kiss me, put his fingers against the waistband of my jeans. I knew I should say something, but I couldn't think of what.

'I was the only one to leave,' he went on. 'I was young. I made my choice. It was the cowardly thing to do.'

There was something comforting about his disconnection, the cleanness of it, the finality. It was, I foolishly thought, so much like my own.

'And you?' he asked. 'Where are you from?'

It was a simple question, and I could have lied. I could have even told the truth, or partial truth. But I didn't say anything. Instead, I reached out and put my hand on the side of his neck, on the complicated network of muscles and veins. I pressed my fingers into his skin and I could feel the cadence of his pulse, the runnel of blood moving between his heart and his brain.

'Let's go inside,' I said.

I didn't understand it then, but I've come to see he was right about his choice to leave his country limiting him forever. We are all confined by what we choose. If I had taken the gift of his question, if I had shown him even the smallest piece of private history, things might be different today. But I was silent and have chosen to remain so for too long. Now even the smallest revelation would seem cataclysmic.

He undressed in my bedroom, and it was then that he told me about the stockyards. I could tell he was afraid, nervous that I might think less of him because of his job. He could not have known how little such a thing would bother me, how simple my desire was. What I wanted was only to watch him undress, to press the nub of my tongue against the salt-rimed ridge of his shoulder, to feel each frangible connection of bone and muscle slipping beneath the fabric of his skin. This was all I wanted from him. At least that's what I told myself.

There wasn't much in my cupboards. I decided on a box of macaroni and cheese, put a pot of water on the stove, and gulped a nice shot of the whiskey. The macaroni was special dinosaur shapes, tiny T. rexes and stegosaurs. When I tossed them into the pot they rolled against one another like slam dancers in a mosh pit. I gave the noodles a good stir, thought about calling Kristof, decided against it. That's the problem with most relationships: They require relating. It's a matter of energy, really, of will and desire, of how much of yourself you're willing to give away.

After I stirred the butter and milk and neon-orange flavoring powder into the tiny dinosaur noodles, I took the entire pot into the living room, put the cushions back in place on the couch, and turned on the TV. The choice was limited, mostly crappy holiday shows: *Christmas in Soap Opera Land, Yuletide Country Jamboree, Miracle on 34th Street*. I worked my way up through the channels until I found an *X-Files* rerun. The show was half over and I didn't have the energy to figure it out. I finished eating, rolled over, and fell asleep.

'Miss Gardner? I know you're in there, Miss Gardner. Open up.'

I opened one eye, squinted toward the front door, and checked my watch. It was just after nine in the morning, and the previous night's whiskey was taking its toll. Moving as slowly as possible so as not to encourage the throbbing in my head, I sat up and ran my fingers through my hair. My first disjointed thought was that it was the cops, but I wasn't so lucky. I recognized Mrs. Jenkins's stocky shoulders and imposing chest through the lace curtain. She put her gloved hand to the window and knocked again. Her little dog yapped from the front yard.

I would have ignored her if I thought it might make her leave, but I had little doubt about her persistence. I pushed myself off the couch and, preparing for the coming tirade, opened the front door.

Mrs. Jenkins was dressed to the holiday nines. She wore one of those Christmas-scene sweatshirts, with Santa's workshop appliquéd across the bulge of her breasts. Santa himself sat just on top of her left nipple, a wide smile stitched across his face. The busy colors made my eyes squirm.

'Miss Gardner,' she whined, 'I'm asking you

nicely. Will you please do something about the walk? My Schatze cannot get through those drifts.'

Opening her arms, she motioned to the creature, who stood on the sidewalk, shivering pathetically.

'It *is* the law, Miss Gardner,' she continued, her eyes widening as she looked over my shoulder and took in the mess behind me.

I closed my eyes and had a quick fantasy involving her neck and my hands, wondering if I could plead justifiable homicide.

'I'll take care of it as soon as I can,' I told her.

'Have you been drinking?' she snapped.

'Yes,' I said, my quota of neighborliness exhausted, 'quite heavily.' Closing the door, I retreated back inside.

I really had very little desire to be accommodating, but once I'm up I have trouble going back to sleep, and I figured getting out in the cold might clear my head. I started a pot of coffee, began a minimal straightening of the mess my visitor had left, slipped into my boots and coat and gloves, and found the snow shovel in the shed in the backyard.

Temperature-wise, things seemed to be on a steady downturn. The sun was out, a rare event at this time of year, and the sky was a vivid blue. But we'd lost a few degrees since the day before. The wind had ebbed to a stiff, steady breeze, and the red needle on the thermometer on my back fence was 20 degrees below the zero mark.

My head still hurt, but I was no longer groggy. As I trudged around to the front I was almost feeling good. The mountains that ring the valley were clear and white, and the air in my lungs was sharp and refined. Even the wire reindeer across the street, with its hollow metal haunches and red globe nose, looked more dignified than usual. Mrs. Jenkins's nativity scene had taken a good beating from the wind. The baby Jesus' crib was overturned and he was lying facedown in the snow. The angel had tumbled off the roof and come to rest in the flower bed, like some bum sleeping off last night's fortified wine.

I was working my way through the last few feet of the walkway, deep in the rhythm of shoveling, when I saw Ivan Popov's black sedan careen down the street. The stereo was cranked up full blast, and the car itself seemed to pulse with the heavy bass beat. Ivan was in the driver's seat. He slid to a stop just behind my Ford, cut the engine, and jumped out. I dropped the shovel and scanned the interior. The man who'd punched me was up front in the passenger seat. When he saw me looking he raised his hand and gave me the finger.

Ivan slogged through the knee-deep powder to the sidewalk, kicking snow onto the newly cleared cement. He was unattractive in the daylight, a younger, jowly version of his father, hulking and fleshy, with a crew cut and bad skin. He wore a hockey jacket, white with red maple leaves. The briefcase was in his right hand, and it knocked against his thigh every time he took a step.

'Where the fuck is it?' he jeered. He came forward until he was just inches from me, coughed up a hefty amount of phlegm, and spit, aiming for my boots and barely missing.

I looked down at the glistening wad. 'I don't know what you're talking about,' I told him.

Ivan leaned in closer. He smelled of stale cigarettes and old sweat. The lock on the briefcase looked like it had been shattered by a gunshot. Ivan flipped the latches and let the case fall open. Sheaves of folded papers tumbled out onto the snow. 'The map, bitch,' he hissed, reaching into his pocket, pulling a neat little nine-millimeter from his coat. He jerked his head toward the house and barked, 'Inside!'

I looked past Ivan to the black sedan and the street beyond. On the other side of the Dairy Queen a car rolled by, then another. I had no intention of moving from that spot in the front yard. Location was all I had going for me, and I wasn't about to give it up. I know the value of witnesses, know what people can do to you when no one's looking.

My hands were down at my sides and I reached up quickly, feeling for Ivan's scrotum through the baggy crotch of his pants. It only took me a second to get a firm grasp on the loose skin, and I twisted it hard to the left and pulled. Ivan muttered something in Russian and jabbed the nine-millimeter into my side.

'I don't have what you're looking for, you little shit,' I told him.

Over Ivan's shoulder I saw the passenger door of the sedan pop open. The big Russian got out and started across the lawn. Ivan raised his free hand and brought his fist down hard on my cheek. I felt the cartilage in my nose compress, the second man's hand on my elbow, then another blow, this time deep in the soft flesh of my abdomen.

Blood was pounding in my ears and I took a breath, bracing my body for more. They didn't hit me again. Someone shoved me hard in the back and my face plowed into the snow.

I picked my head up and saw Mrs. Jenkins. 'Get!' she was yelling, as if to a pack of wild dogs. She brandished her cordless phone like a weapon. 'I mean it,' she wailed from her porch. 'I'll call the police!' I could hear Schatze howling from the other side of the screen door.

Ivan stared at her, curling his lips back into a mean smile. The other Russian took a step back and clapped his gloves together.

'I'm not finished with you,' Ivan hissed. Then they both headed across the yard to the waiting sedan.

From where I lay I had a good view of Mrs. Jenkins's ankles as she struggled toward me. She was wearing house slippers without socks, and her skin was loose and pale, laced with blue veins.

'No good,' she wheezed, the last traces of calm leaving her, 'no good.' When she put her hand on my arm to help me up, I could feel her entire body shaking.

'It's okay,' I told her, staggering up, brushing loose snow from my pants.

She wagged her head. Her breath was sour with fear, her cheeks flushed bright pink.

'Really. It's okay. You should go inside.'

'What a mess,' she mumbled.

I put my hand to my nose and felt a warm smear

of blood. The ground where I had fallen was flecked with pink clots. Bennett's briefcase lay open in the snow, its contents fluttering like wounded butterflies. I leaned over, picked one of the papers up, unfolded it.

'Maps,' Mrs. Jenkins remarked, shuddering slightly. She wrapped her arms tight around her chest and turned to go inside.

I nodded to myself. There must have been at least two dozen of them, each marked with rivers and names, with the concentric circles of topography. I bent down, gathered the maps, and piled them back into the case. All the while I was thinking of Ivan and the woman, looking for something I didn't have. I was thinking of Clay Bennett, what someone had done to him, what they might do to me. Then I heard Amos. What he'd said at Charlie's suddenly seemed a little less insane. *They say she stabbed him, but I bet she ain't the one done it.*

Dusting the snow from my pants, I took the maps inside, called Darwin, and asked her to meet me out at the dealership. I wanted to get rid of the Jeep and find Amos. I needed some answers I thought he might have.

# Seven

The drive across the valley with the Jeep's broken window was long and cold. The wind had burnished the streets slick as the surface of a skating rink, and the highway was lined with the carcasses of deserted cars. Even in the weather-handling Cherokee I had to creep along. It was not yet noon, and already there was a feeling of imminent dusk. Smoke from the mill hung in dark ribbons against the mountains. Winter had settled in, with no intention of leaving anytime soon.

There are places where it's easy to deny the passage of time, where nothing ever dies and people grow lulled and stupefied like hens readied for the chopping block. Montana is not one of those places. Here it's impossible to turn away from the annual Armageddon of winter. Sometime in October the trees change and the streets are washed with gold currents of leaves. Then one night the frost comes, settling like cold, nocturnal sunshine, and only those plants sheltered by the shadow of the house survive. About a week later, everything goes.

Navigating the snowy streets with the numbing wind on my face, I felt an acute sense of loss at the absence of color, the monotonous gray of snow and sky. Winter seemed like a willful presence, an unwelcome guest, a mother-in-law who had unpacked her bags and settled in for a prolonged stay.

Darwin was waiting for me at the dealership. I could see her inside talking to Flip and the lot manager, a guy named Jan Jorgenson. Behind the wide windows of the showroom, new cars were arrayed like sugary pastries in a bakery case. Chrome hubcaps and buffed finishes shone seductively under the glare of the spotlights.

I honked my horn to let them know I was there. Then I drove the Jeep around to the back of the dealership, parked it in the chain-linked enclosure where they kept the repos, and went in through the garage entrance.

Jan was talking when I stepped into the showroom, his voice low and solemn. '. . . hard-luck story – I heard him say, before he looked up at me and his voice broke off.

'You talking about Flip?' I smiled.

Flip winked amiably. I could tell he'd slipped into a pre-Christmas coma. His eyes were rimmed with dark circles and his hair stood out at odd angles from his head. 'You try playing Santa to five kids.' He shrugged, gesturing to Jan. 'Actually, we were talking about Clayton Bennett.'

'What about him?'

Jan spoke up. 'I was just reminding Flip how it was Bennett who crashed his plane up the Bitterroot sometime back in the late fifties. Fifty-eight, maybe?'

'He was Air Force Reserve,' Flip said. 'Went

down in an old training plane in one of those freak spring storms up over the mountains.'

'That *is* hard luck,' I agreed.

'That's not the half of it,' Flip continued. 'They gave him up for dead right away. Sent a death certificate to his wife and everything.'

Jan broke in. 'The way I remember it there wasn't much of a search, I suppose on account of the weather, though it seems to me it cleared up within a couple of days. I remember we thought it kind of strange. I was working out at Johnson-Belle Field then, loading planes for a cargo company. I remember the paper saying they were flying out of Fairchild to look for him. But according to our pilots there was no one in the air. They never did find the plane.'

'So what happened?' I asked.

Jan looked at Flip. 'How long was it? A couple of months, right?'

'Two months, I think,' Flip agreed.

'Whatever, one day about two months after he went down, Bennett walked out of the woods. A little worse for wear, but alive.'

We all fell silent for a moment, contemplating Bennett's story. Finally, Flip clapped his hands together. 'Well,' he said. 'I hear you've got some bad news for us.'

I nodded. 'Broken window.'

Flip smiled. 'It could be worse.'

After I'd filled out the regular paperwork and Flip had paid me, I talked Darwin into heading downtown with me to Al and Vic's, one of Amos's favorite watering holes. My visits from Ivan and the woman were still fresh in my mind, and I was glad to have Darwin along. The bartenders at Al and Vic's are all over sixty with names like Monte and Stu, and they still know how to make manhattans and old-fashioneds. Walking through the door is like stepping into a time machine. Even the television, a brand-new RCA set, has been adjusted so it only shows black-and-white, as if color might be an insult to the regular customers. Best of all, a double shot in a pint glass only costs $2.50.

We parked in front of the Double Front, bunched the collars of our coats tightly around our necks, and scrambled across the street. The cold had brought everyone inside, and we were lucky to get the last free stools at the old wood bar. There was no sign of Amos, but I saw Kristof bent over the pool table in the back of the bar. He was racking the balls, his back to me. I hunched down behind Darwin, not hiding, really, just not in the mood to explain why I hadn't returned his call.

Darwin went to the sandwich counter next door and got us some burgers, and we sat for a while without speaking and soaked up the patter around us, the soft noise Monte's shoes made on the worn floor as he shuffled back and forth from the well to the cash register, the clicking of pool balls. I was halfway through my burger and a bottle of Pabst Blue Ribbon when Darwin nudged me.

'Your boyfriend's here,' she said, tilting her head toward the back of the bar.

I looked past her and watched Kristof bend at the waist and sight down his cue. He slid the tapered stick back and forth with his right hand and hit the cue ball cleanly, sinking two balls.

'He's not my boyfriend,' I told her.

'Uh-huh. You know what Flip says: "If it looks like shit and smells like shit—" '

'He's not my boyfriend.' I downed the last of my beer and pushed the empty bottle across the bar, glaring at her reflection in the mirror.

Darwin cleared her throat loudly, fiddled with a Virginia Slim.

I signaled for a second round. Monte brought the drinks, and I paid him and lit a cigarette. 'You seen Amos around today?' I asked, when he brought my change.

He bent across the bar, flipping his lighter open for Darwin. 'Kinda early. He generally starts his day over at Charlie's. Comes in here around happy hour.'

Darwin inhaled, flashed Monte a gracious smile, and sat back on her stool. 'What you asking about that freak for, anyway?'

I shrugged and fell silent for half a dozen heartbeats.

'You got something goin' on you want to tell me about?'

'Just looking for information.'

Darwin knit her eyebrows together, pursed her lips. 'Lookin' for trouble, maybe, if Amos is involved.'

I rolled my coal against the lip of the ashtray. 'Too late to go looking,' I told her. 'I've already been found.'

'What's that s'posed to mean?'

'Nothing good,' I said, pushing myself off my stool, heading for the back.

I had to walk right by the pool table to get to the bathroom. Kristof was racking a new game and I squeezed past him without saying anything. When I came out he was waiting for me, his right hand wrapped around his pool cue. Balancing the stick on its rubber end piece, he twisted it back and forth. His fingers on the wood were strong and delicate at the same time.

'You're not working today?' I asked.

'Late lunch break.'

'You want to come over later?'

'Okay.' He nodded.

Out of the corner of my eye I could see Darwin watching us. 'Around eight,' I told him, and turned and walked back to the bar.

'No, sir,' Darwin said, shaking her head, slipping into her coat. 'I would definitely say he is not your boyfriend. Definitely.'

'Where you going?' I asked.

'Amvets,' she explained, pointing her thumb to the door. 'Got a rehearsal for the Christmas show. You want me to drop you off at home?'

I checked my watch. 'No, thanks. I'm gonna head over to Charlie's.'

She buttoned her coat and looked up at me, suddenly dead serious. 'You need my help?' she asked.

I shook my head.

'Trouble,' Darwin mumbled. Then she glanced back at Kristof. 'You ever wonder what he sees in you, why he sticks around?'

I shrugged. 'Oldest reason there is, I guess.'

'The boy's a glutton for punishment,' she said, and we both stepped out into the frigid air.

It was just a few short blocks from Al and Vic's over to Charlie's. I was dressed for the weather, clunky Sorel pac boots, down coat, watch cap, and long underwear, but the cold was still winning. Every inch of exposed skin was stinging when I walked through the door and into the warmth of the bar.

Inside, it was the usual crowd, slumming students and lowlifes, with a few respectable drinkers thrown in, doctors and lawyers and even the occasional cop out for a late lunch at the Dinosaur Café. With the university on its Christmas break, the student presence was lower than normal. The kids who were there had commandeered the sound system. Bob Marley blared from the speakers.

Working my way toward the bar, I scanned the smoke-cloaked crowd for Amos. I recognized Bill Jackson, the owner of the Super Six Motel, his back hunched over one of the poker machines. His dog Dogin, a crazy Blue Heeler prone to fits of violence, was curled at Bill's side, his eyes narrow slits, his body deceptively limp. When the dog spotted me, his ears went up. He shifted onto his paws and curled his lips back over his teeth.

The last thing I wanted was a scuffle with the Blue Heeler, so, strapping on my most relaxed smile, I backed around the dog. 'Good boy,' I said cheerfully. Unconvinced of his own virtue, Dogin inched down onto his stomach, snarling. I elbowed my way to the bar and ordered a Moose Drool.

It was about half an hour and two drinks later when Amos showed up. The front door of Charlie's swung open and cold air wafted through the bar. I looked up to see Amos's face lurching through the crowd.

'Buy you a beer?' I asked when Amos threw himself down on the stool next to mine.

He looked behind him like a man being pursued by rabid dogs. His eyes darted over the crowd. 'Huh?'

'Can . . . I . . . buy . . . you . . . a . . . beer?'

'Yeah, sure.' He pulled a bag of loose tobacco from his coat and started to roll a cigarette. His hands were shaking like an old man's. Tobacco spilled onto the bar.

I offered him one of my Parliaments and he flashed me a sheepish grin. 'Fuckin' hands are half froze,' he stammered.

He had dyed his hair since I had last seen him. The spikes alternated from red to green. 'You like it?' he asked, fingering the tips of his Mohawk.

'Not particularly,' I told him, waving the bartender over, ordering two beers.

'Red and green. You know, for Christmas. Everyone down at the station thinks it's great.'

I took a sip of beer and felt Amos's hand slide across my thigh. 'You look pretty tonight,' he whispered. 'We could go back to my place. You know, a little holiday cheer.'

'You're disgusting,' I told him, picking his sweaty hand from my pant leg.

74

The bartender set two Rainiers in front of us and I watched Amos guzzle half the bottle.

'I guess they caught those two Indians,' I said cautiously, trying to ease my way into conversation. Amos was a lot like Bill Jackson's Blue Heeler in that you never really knew what might set him off.

He nodded, his eyes focused on some faraway point. I was hoping he'd repeat the theory he'd voiced the other night, something about it being someone besides Tina who'd done the killing. But he sat there like a stone, the muscle in his jaw flexing in and out.

'So?' I asked, shifting my approach, adding a hint of jest to my voice. 'You figure out who it was killed Bennett?'

Amos slammed the Rainier down on the bar and looked over his shoulder again. 'What are you asking me that for?' he snarled.

I reached out and touched his shoulder, smiled. 'Hey, man,' I said calmly. 'Just giving you a hard time. I must have misheard you.'

'Well, you did,' he stammered, picking nervously at the label on his Rainier bottle. 'I didn't see nothing.' Lifting the beer to his lips, he chugged down the remaining half of the contents, zipped his coat up to his chin, and made a beeline for the back door.

It was bizarre behavior even for Amos. Normally he clung to me like burrs to a dog's coat. His brightly hued Mohawk bobbed through the crowd, disappearing into the alcove that housed the bathrooms and the rear door. I got up and followed him toward the pool tables and Charlie's old oak back bar. A few customers were sitting on the empty coolers and mirrored liquor shelves.

As I passed the pool tables I did a double take. Nick Popov's wife, Vera, the one who had served us tea at the Hot Springs place, and a man about twenty years her junior were propped up against a section of the old mirror. Vera had on black pumps and a black dress with pearly buttons up the front and a busy pattern of little white flowers. Her brown hair was done up in meticulous curls and she was sitting turned toward the man, with her right leg bent and tucked under her. Her left foot dangled in midair and her skirt was hiked up to reveal a smooth expanse of thigh. Their heads were bent toward each other, and over the ear-numbing reggae I could hear her laughing while he spoke.

*I should have known better,* I remembered Nick saying. I gave Vera and her friend one last glance and slipped through the narrow back corridor, between the bathrooms and the cramped kitchen. Bracing myself for the cold, I put my hand on the greasy doorknob and stepped out into the alley.

After the warmth of the bar, the outside air was especially biting. The potholed asphalt was slick with frozen sludge and grease. I had to step carefully to keep my balance. Christ, I thought, pulling my watch cap tight over my ears and buttoning the top flap of my parka. I wasn't relishing the idea of walking home and thought I'd head back to Al and Vic's, see if Kristof might still be there.

I was passing the corner of the building when I lost my footing. One second I was upright, and the next something knocked against my right shin, sending my nose slamming into an ice-crusted pool of stinking alley water. I flattened my palms against the broken blacktop and pushed myself onto my knees, trying to regain my bearings. There was a sharp pain above my right eye. I put my finger to my face and felt torn skin, a sticky stain of blood.

'Bad fall,' a woman's voice said from above me. 'You must have tripped.'

I knew without turning who she was, knew it was her foot I'd felt on my shin and that it was no accident. My heart flipflopped in the cage of my ribs. 'Whatever it is you want, I don't have it and I can't get it,' I told her, struggling onto all fours. I shifted my weight onto my heels and tried to stand. The sole of her boot pressed into my spine, holding me down.

I craned my head around to get a good look at her. She had a few years on me, mid-thirties or early forties, with a pocked face and stringy brown hair. Her frame was tall and bulky, not fat but muscular, with thick shoulders. The cold didn't seem to bother her. She was wearing a worn leather biker's jacket and black jeans. Everything about her reminded me of the more unpleasant aspects of my life before: bags of stale Cheetos, day-old coffee, egg rolls under the red light of a gas station heat lamp, greasy fingers stained with salt, the acrid smell of clothes worn one too many times.

'You need to talk to Ivan Popov,' I said. 'This is something about a map, right?'

'Who?'

'Russian car thief.' I coughed, thinking I could at least buy myself some time. 'Got a chop shop out in East Missoula. Old Texaco station off the highway.'

I was wearing a turtleneck and she bent down, pulled the knit fabric away from my skin, and ran her finger along the cut she'd left the day before. 'Seems like you have a thing for Eastern Europeans,' she snarled, her breath on my ear. Her jacket fell open, revealing a fading tattoo below her right collarbone, a red dragon with the name *Josie* in thick black ink.

'What are you talking about?' I asked, wrenching myself away from her.

She reached into her coat and drew a shiny Polaroid from the inside pocket. Her smile was a broad white sickle. 'Your boyfriend,' she said, letting the photograph fall from her hand, pushing my face to the ground. 'I'm sure you would hate it if something were to happen to him.'

I opened my eyes wide and stared at the picture. It was hastily taken, slightly out of focus. Still, I recognized the subject. There was my house, bleak and washed-out against the snowy background. There was my porch, the paint on the steps peeling to bare wood, the mailbox propped open. And there was Kristof, his hand on the railing, his head tilted slightly downward, his cheeks colored by the cold.

'Thanks for the information,' I heard her say.

'I'll let you know how things work out. With this Ivan.' Then she lifted her boot from my back, turned toward the mouth of the alley, and disappeared.

# Eight

I didn't need a repeat visit from Josie the dragon lady to know how things would work out with Ivan. The two of them were both looking for the same thing, and even if Ivan had found the map, it hardly seemed likely he'd be willing to share. No doubt I'd see Josie again soon, and I figured she wouldn't be so pleasant at our third encounter.

I wrested my eyes from the Polaroid of Kristof, shoved it into my pocket, and stood up carefully. It was one thing to have gotten myself mixed up in Josie and Ivan and Bennett's little triangle. Now Kristof was involved. I didn't feel comfortable thinking his well-being was somehow in my hands.

The pavement spun out beneath me and I leaned up against the brick wall, regaining my balance. I took one long inhalation, then another, watching my breath roil out and disperse. I could feel caked grime on my face, warm blood from when I'd fallen. Pushing myself off the wall, I made my way back into Charlie's and headed for the ladies' room.

It was no more than ten feet from the back door to the bathrooms. From the small hallway I could see Vera Popov, still posed on the bar like a cheap calendar model: back straight, breasts high, leg tucked under her. The kid was gone and Vera was scanning the crowd like a wolf ogling a herd of cattle. I turned my head away from her to put my hand on the door to the bathroom, and a pair of eyes locked on mine. The face they belonged to was less youthful than when I'd last seen it, but I recognized Jeff Riley's features all the same. Christ, I thought, as I ducked my head, avoiding his gaze, just what I need. I stepped into the bathroom, locked the door behind me, and turned the hot tap on as far as it would go.

I knew he'd be waiting when I came out, and I took my time washing my face, dabbing at the front of my coat with a paper towel. With my hair tucked up into my watch cap I looked almost presentable when I emerged.

Riley had taken a stool at the back bar, close to the bathrooms. He dipped his head when I stepped through the door, made a small nod of acknowledgment. 'You okay?'

I looked over at him, his perfect white teeth, his lips curling into a paternal smile, and my childhood came racing back to me like a cutthroat curving upstream.

The night my mother shot my father was not the first time my parents had argued. Some of my earliest memories were of minor acts of violence heard through my bedroom walls. The crash of china on Sheetrock. The sounds of two people tussling. Breathless sobbing. And there were subtler forms of acrimony. The clothes my mother wore.

Thin bands that crisscrossed her back, showed the entire length of her spine, the swell of her shoulders. The way she enjoyed talking to men at parties, the way her throat rose up, milky and sculpted, when she threw her head back and laughed.

The day after my father was shot a social worker took me downtown to the police station and put me in a yellow room with ratty dolls and copies of *Highlights* magazine. It was like the waiting room at the doctor's office, but worse. I had a bottle of pink nail polish in my pocket from the slumber party, and I painted each finger while I waited.

By the time they came in to question me I had my story all worked out. I didn't tell them a thing. I hated my mother for what she had done, hated her even before she shot him. But I would not take sides in my parents' struggle. The young detective they sent to talk to me was handsome in the way teen singing idols are. I will always remember his disappointed face in the corridor when he left, his skin crosshatched by the wired glass that divided him from me.

The most remarkable thing about small towns is the uncommonly slow rate of change. Chances are your second-grade desk has stayed in its place and the hearts and arrows you carved in the wood are still there, the boy you carved them for still working at his father's convenience store off the interstate. Most faces are familiar, even if they've lost all context: the high-school quarterback, let's say, sallow-cheeked now, hanging off the bar.

So it was no surprise to see Riley again. I'd been

expecting to run into him since I'd been back. The young detective had grown older, predictably, but he was still handsome in a Western sort of way. Tall and lanky, clean-shaven and clean-cut, he was a modern-day Roy Rogers. Mid-forties, easing his way toward a well-preserved old age. His face, beneath a fine layer of stubble, was ruddy and wholesome. It was a 'yes, ma'am' kind of face: dutiful, polite, not unkind. He was dressed in street clothes: tan cowboy boots, jeans, a worn black Carhartt jacket.

I had a less-than-stellar record after the shooting, and Riley had taken a special interest in me. Looking back, I'm sure he had only good intentions, but at the time I hated him. I hated the police youth foundation circus tickets, the charity handouts. I remember he came to the high school once when they were going to suspend me. He talked the administration into giving me another chance, and I despised him for it, despised the serious, self-righteous way in which he talked to me.

I stared at him now, forgetting the question he'd asked, forgetting it was my turn to speak.

'You okay?' he asked again.

I nodded. 'Yeah.'

The thing to remember about cops is that they'll always make you feel like you've done something wrong even when you haven't. Riley was no different. He paused for a moment, checking me over.

'Join me for a bite to eat?' he said, his voice just slightly patronizing. He motioned to a half-eaten sandwich and a bowl of gumbo.

'I'm not hungry.'

Riley blinked once, then again, his gaze steady on my face. 'For old times' sake,' he told me.

I understood this wasn't a request, wasn't something I had a choice in.

'It's good to see you, Meg,' he said, finally.

I had more important things to worry about and thought briefly of ducking out the back door; then I decided I might as well get whatever conversation he wanted to have over with. There's no dodging people in a town as small as Missoula. I knew he'd track me down sooner or later, so I found a stool across from him, shrugged out of my coat and ordered a cup of coffee.

'Can I get you something to eat?' he asked again.

I shook my head. 'I hear you've been promoted.'

'Police chief,' he said. A spoonful of gumbo hovered midway to his mouth. 'What have you been up to?'

I shrugged. 'Did some time down in New Mexico.'

'Christ, Meg.' Riley sighed. 'You're smarter than that.' He spooned the gumbo into his mouth, swallowed, and tilted his head toward the back door. 'What happened?'

I shrugged again. I wasn't trying to irritate him, it's just not in my nature to be helpful to the authorities. I've been on their bad side too many times.

'You in some kind of trouble?' He waved his spoon to indicate my face.

I took another sip of the coffee. Flip always says

the cops are our friends. I'm not so sure about that, but I couldn't really see the good in lying.

'I've been working for Flip Watkins,' I told him. 'Looks like I pissed someone off.'

'You're doing repo work?'

I nodded. 'People weren't exactly lining up to give me a job.'

Riley smiled and I could almost hear his cop mind passing judgment on me: liar, criminal, low-life. 'You want to tell me who jumped you?'

'No, thanks. It comes with the territory.' I downed the last of my coffee and stood up, slipping into my coat. 'I assume I'm free to go?'

The police chief nodded, stood up. 'What happened in New Mexico?' he asked when I moved to step past him.

'Nothing I'm proud of. Listen, no more playing daddy, okay? It's my life. I'll work it out.'

'If you ever need anything,' Riley said, laying his palm on my shoulder, 'you know I'm always here for you.'

'Right.' I turned to go, then stopped myself. 'You know, there *is* something I've been wondering about. That Red Deer woman. Things aren't looking too rosy for her, are they?'

He raised his eyebrows, puzzled, 'No. Why do you ask?'

'Old times, you know. It just got me thinking.'

It was during the last few years I spent at home that my mother undertook her great transformation. She was extremely public in her newfound passion. She took to crossing herself in the supermarket, genuflecting while in line at the bank. She whispered the Lord's Prayer before every meal. *Our Father, who art in heaven,* she would say, and I would watch her eyes grow misty with forced tears. At night I would hear her in her room, confessing her sins. *Forgive me,* she would say, *for things I have done and left undone.*

It was a cold walk home from Charlie's, solitary as a trek across some lifeless planet. The mountains loomed like the pale shoulders of naked giants. Birds swarmed like black stars above the bare branches of trees.

All the way down Higgins and across the bridge with the Clark Fork frozen beneath me, I thought about Tina Red Deer, my mind churning like a spade in untilled dirt. I thought about the clanging doors of the jail, the familiar squeal of metal on metal. There are habits to incarceration. The long walk to the shower, rubber sandals slapping against waxed linoleum. The repetition of labor, hands folding and refolding each sheet. And meals, each tray nestled into the next like lovers.

When they brought me in all those years earlier and asked me about my parents it was Riley who had questioned me. Riley, a still-young detective. It was Riley who had stood in our front hall blushing at my mother's gaze, who would later write the words ACCIDENTAL SHOOTING on the piece of paper that would spare my mother from incarceration. And it was with Riley that I had committed my first sins of omission.

I didn't tell him about my mother, the way she could make my father shrink before her. I didn't tell him about the long trips my father made to the reservation, the way my mother would say the word *squaw* as if it were live ammunition. And I didn't tell him about the woman who had come to the house. She had stood on the porch the day before my father was shot. Her hair was slick and black, as if it had been polished. A shiny braid hung down her back. She was the first woman I had ever seen who was more beautiful than my mother. Her legs were muscular and her hands were like delicate birds.

There was a child with her, a little girl about my age, maybe a year or two older. She held the woman's hand in a way that made me understand they were mother and daughter. I kneeled on the couch with my face pressed to the glass of the front window, and the girl and I contemplated each other as if we were rivals.

# Nine

Darkness came on fast and early that afternoon. By the time I got home, the sky to the west of the valley was striped with wide red welts. The house was cold. Mrs. Carter's old furnace seemed to be pumping out just enough heat to keep the pipes unfrozen. The wind roared out of the canyon and shuddered against the window of my bedroom, glazing the panes with ice. I took a long hot shower and put on some thermal underwear, a pair of wool pants, and a thick wool sweater. Padding into the living room, I slid the Polaroid of Kristof from the pocket of my coat, switched a lamp on, and held the picture under the bulb.

When I was a child I overheard my father tell one of his friends that there were worse things than dying. I didn't know what he meant, exactly, but my little mind took the phrase in and wouldn't let go. For years I must have pondered the possibilities. I could think of nothing worse than dying.

My hands were shaking. I lit a cigarette and laid the picture on the arm of my couch. She had watched him, I thought, and he hadn't known. I went to the window and looked out across the empty street, trying to guess where she might have stood. In the shadow of my neighbor's shrubs, maybe, the tall ones that bloom yellow in late summer.

Think of heat sizzling against the reservoir of your oculus, or your fingernails peeled back to the pith, your skin tender and pulpy like the exposed flesh of an orange. Think of all the crude manifestations of torture: thumbscrews, cattle prods, the breathless panic of drowning enacted upon you over and over again. Think of the miracle of your body and all it can endure. You could survive these things and worse. You could come out on the other side of this unspeakable pain and still be grateful for the air whistling in your lungs.

The first time I kissed him, Kristof put his finger on a puckered scar on my face, on the discolored rift where torn cells had knit themselves into a mimicry of skin. Later, after I had undressed, he found others, a long sickle on my calf, a raised sunburst on my thigh, a fading cicatrix on my elbow with its neat border of stitch marks. Of course he could not have known the history of these brands. He could not have guessed which was a relic of a playground fall, which a souvenir of betrayal. Yet there was something obscene about his tongue against these tiny fissures, something indecent about the intimacy of it. It was almost as if, in the tangy salt of my sweat, he could taste each moment of damage.

Yes, I thought, my father was right. There are things that are worse than dying, things that have nothing to do with the hard pellicle of your own flesh.

What if they took the bones of another's hand and crushed them? What if they made you watch? Would you think of those hands as they had been, the flutter of the fingers against your pelvis, the bloodless imprint of the thumb on your inner thigh, the palms closing around your breast? If they took a knife to the neck, to the spot where you had once counted the metered pulse of the heart, would you replay the incision again and again? Would it be an introduction, an induction, a doorway opening to the leering face of grief?

Slipping into my Sorels and coat, I found Mrs. Carter's twenty-two and headed for the door.

It was just before eight when I cut through downtown and cruised out between the wind-sheared flanks of Hellgate Canyon. I was hoping to make amends with Ivan, hoping he'd at least take a friendly warning and give me some information in return. Like what, exactly, Josie was looking for, and why.

The clouds had dissipated some and it was a fairly clear night. Out in the canyon the shadow of Mount Jumbo loomed large, blocking out the stars, the thick crescent of the moon. Tucked between two mountains, East Missoula was at least ten degrees colder than the open bowl of the valley. The snow-blown neighborhoods glowed under orange streetlamps. Televisions flickered behind windows. Strands of Christmas lights shivered in the wind. Rusted skeletons of cars and castaway household appliances dotted lawns like flotsam strewn across a beach.

I spotted Ivan's yellow Camaro, the one Darwin and I had been sent to repossess, parked in front of what had once been the East Missoula Texaco station. The windows of the old garage were whitewashed and I couldn't see inside, but I could see that the lights were on. The Camaro, its windshield clouded with frost, was the only car in the lot. Easing off the street, I pulled up next to the derelict pumps and cut the truck's engine.

A radio was playing somewhere inside the garage, filtering out into the parking lot. A local rock station belted out its call letters, then faded into an old Quiet Riot song. I made my way to the front door and knocked, pounding until my knuckles hurt. 'Ivan!' I yelled.

I waited a few seconds and knocked again, cupped my hands around my eyes, and tried to peer in through the whitewashed pane. There was a tiny scratch in the paint just to the left of the door and I could see a slice of the interior. An old glass counter. Part of a cash register. An ashtray heaped with cigarette butts and an empty Stolichnaya bottle.

Still getting no answer, I turned and headed around toward the back of the building, searching for a way in.

The drifts behind the garage were muddled and pocked with the remnants of footprints. I sank my boots into the feathery snow and picked my way through brush and weeds. The music was louder back here, and when I finally reached the rear entrance I understood why. The back door stood ajar, propped open by a heavy drift that had accumulated on the threshold. I glanced around, suddenly struck by the sensation that I might not be alone, then felt for the stiff shape of the twenty-two in my pocket and stepped inside.

It was warm in the garage. The heat had been cranked up enough to accommodate the open door. The smells of paint and grease and gasoline were overwhelming.

'Ivan!' I called. There was no response.

The skeleton of an unrecognizable car teetered high above me on a hydraulic lift. A pile of hubcaps filled one corner like wrecked flying saucers. I located the radio, crossed to the shelf that held it, and switched it off, plunging the garage into blessed silence.

'Ivan!' I tried one more time. Nothing.

And then I saw him. He was like a mirage, a flash viewed from the corner of the eye that disappears when you look at it full on. It was his hand I noticed, the whiteness of it against the dirty concrete floor. The fingers were draped over the side of one of the mechanic's pits, and at first I thought he was grappling to pull himself up. But as I made my way closer, it became more and more evident that that was not his intent.

Ivan was dressed perfectly for the occasion, as if he had known beforehand that he would be forever remembered in what he chose to wear that day. He had on a dark suit and a pink shirt. A pale blue tie hung snugly around his neck. One hand was raised, the other twisted behind him. His knees were drawn slightly up toward his chest. The mechanic's pit was just the right size and depth to hold him, like a coffin that had been made to measure.

I squatted down for a closer look. His eyes were open wide, and the overhead lights reflected in his irises like two bright beads. A black gash stretched across his throat like a mock smile. Whoever had cut him had done so meticulously. His head was tilted back in such a way that, except for a few stray splashes, his shirt and tie were relatively spotless. The blood had flowed down the side of his neck in two neat lines and pooled beneath his shoulder blades.

I've always been a sucker for bad slasher films. Death by chain saw. Death by machete. Death by pitchfork. I like how neatly these movies order violence, how easy it is to tell which character is going to die. And even though you separate yourself early on from the cheerleader who gives her virginity up too easily, it still fills you with fear when you realize she is about to lose her head. I've given these movies a lot of thought, and I've come to believe that the heavy-handed moral distinctions serve a grand purpose. They allow you to truly dislike a character, to lose all trace of pity or outrage. With these ancillary emotions out of the way, you can experience the reign of terror in all its splendor.

And I like the unwritten rules, the basement you should never check, the window you should never look through, the strange noise you must never investigate. And then the last bang of stupidity: the girl in her nightgown slowly descending the stairs, the camera homed in on her nipples silhouetted beneath the cotton bodice. Or the would-be hero sinking to his knees beside the newly dead villain. Pan to the slow beat of the carotid artery. Pan to the fingers fluttering, the imminent resurrection of evil.

There's a kind of perverse pleasure in the omniscient power of being the observer. You know who's lurking at the bottom of the stairs. The hundred-plus other people around you in the dark know. There's a collective gasp. Thighs shift against the edges of seats. And everyone keeps on watching.

The problem with real life, as most people will tell you, is that you don't have all the angles covered. There's no zoom lens on the back door, no overhead camera. Every shot is point-of-view, and so you muddle on into the unknown.

It took a second for the full impact of the situation to sink in. My legs went rubbery and I felt my stomach rise up into the back of my throat. I sat down on a stack of truck tires and lit a cigarette, trying to stay calm. Ivan's unmoving gaze was fixed on a position just beyond my head. If I squinted I could almost imagine he was looking right at me, as if we were conversing. I stared at the indentation in his skull, squashed my cigarette, and lit another. I could smell the thick odor of his blood over the paint and gas fumes.

'Hey, Ivan,' I said, startling myself with my own voice. 'You come out here all alone?'

I got up from my stack of tires and made a quick sweep of the garage. I had seen Ivan's everyday attire, and the Russian was dressed far too nicely for a trip to the garage. In fact, his clothes were almost more unusual than what had been done to him. In Missoula, even the Mormons dress down. Even lawyers, preachers, stockbrokers. Even wanna-be Russian gangsters. About the only people who wear suits are undertakers.

I ducked into the little room off the front of the garage, the one I'd seen when I'd peered in the front window. Stools were set up around the old counter. There was the empty Stoli bottle I'd glimpsed. Two glasses sat beside it, one marked with a bright red butterfly of lipstick. A woman had been here.

My first thought was that it was Josie. But that didn't explain Ivan's clothes. And why would he have shared a bottle of vodka with her? Why would she have wasted precious time drinking? No, I told myself. Josie may have been here, but it was some other woman's lipstick on the glass. The most logical explanation was that Ivan had been on a date. Why else the fancy suit, the slick black shoes, useless in winter? I crushed my cigarette with my heel. Then, thinking it better not to leave any traces of my presence, I leaned down and reached for the butt.

I was standing up when I saw it, a flash of tastelessness tucked under the shelf that held the old cash register. A small purse, red satin with gold beads stitched on the fabric in a stylized pattern of flowers, like something Darwin would own. I pulled the bag out and popped the clasp, peered inside. Eyeliner. Blush. Eye shadow in a wretched shade of purple. Cigarettes. A tube of lipstick called Carmine Passion, the shade a match to the one left on the rim of the vodka glass.

I dug through the cosmetics, hoping to find a

wallet, a driver's license, a credit card, anything. Several crumpled twenty-dollar bills swam in the sea of makeup brushes and nail files. I pulled a small glass bottle out and read the label. The words were Russian, the letters powder blue over a background of pink and white flowers. A gift from Ivan? I took the little gold top off the bottle, sniffed the contents. Even Russian perfume was second-rate.

I set the bottle aside, dug farther into the purse. My fingers caught on a jumble of keys and I pulled them out, laid them on the counter. On the chain was a rabbit's foot, the fur dyed to a bright vivid pink. A small tag dangled from the foot, a shiny piece of copper with the word VERA stamped into it. Suddenly the perfume made sense.

My mother wore perfume when I was a girl. White Shoulders. The cheap stuff, she always used to say, a dead giveaway of her wheat farmer origins. Even when she was wealthy enough to afford better she kept wearing it. I remember other little bottles of amber liquid strewn across the top of her dresser, more expensive fragrances that went unused. She tried to explain to me one day, said something about a woman's identity, something about smell and familiarity, something I didn't quite believe.

It wasn't until later that I came to understand the power of fragrance, how smell was the sense that could most easily transport you. When I worked in the laundry room in New Mexico, I would plunge my face into the steaming sheets when they came out of the dryer. It was like childhood, that smell of hot cotton, like the warm sheets my mother would put on my bed in the wintertime. And sometimes, when the wind came to us from the desert smelling of pine or sage, I would stand in the yard and inhale. I would think of my father, of hunting with him on the Rocky Mountain Front, of a herd of antelope I once saw pour over a ridge, their movements precise as an army's. A river of them, a great wave cresting the brown hill, turning all at once toward the east, moving on.

So I understood why Vera would carry bad Russian perfume in her purse. What I didn't understand was how the handbag came to be left behind. If there's one thing a woman doesn't forget it's her purse. I studied the gaudy bag, tried to envision their evening. She would have to have hurried to make it here from Charlie's after a quick goodbye to the kid I'd seen her talking to. Nick Popov was right, he should have known better. And here she had been, with his own son.

And then what? A trip to the bathroom? Something that got her outside. And when she came back what had she seen? Something to make her leave her purse, something that sent her away in a hurry. Dead Ivan, maybe. Or maybe she was the one who killed him, though this seemed unlikely.

A truck whooshed by on the street outside the garage, its jake brakes mewling like a beached whale. I looked up, goose bumps rising on my arms, and watched the headlights skate across the whitewashed windows. You've overstayed your welcome, I told myself. I stuffed the contents of Vera's purse back into the red bag, slipped it under my arm, and headed out through the garage.

*

97

The ride back through town was slow going. The wind kept up a sustained howl. The snow on the roads had been hard-packed to slick ice. A smoky river of dry powder writhed across the blacktop. Just off the Van Buren Street bridge, I noticed a blue Volkswagen, overturned and half buried in a drift. What few people were out were cloaked in scarves and hats.

Turning the radio on, I scanned the stations for a temperature. The last reading at the airport was 23 degrees below zero. Even if you grew up here, if you spent each winter of your life battling the cold, you'd never get used to it. As far as hospitality for the human organism is concerned, we might as well have been on Mars.

I glanced at the red bag on the seat next to me, thought about Vera laughing with the kid in Charlie's, her thigh perfect as sculpted stone, seductive. And I thought about the other woman, the red dragon rippling across her chest. I had given Ivan to her, and now he was dead.

# Ten

All the way back down the canyon I could smell Ivan on me. I lowered both windows and lit one cigarette after another, trying to mask the scent. The odor of death loitered in my nostrils, in each fiber of my clothing. I couldn't shake the picture of Kristof, the thought of Josie watching him. I stopped at the red light on Higgins, then breezed through the intersection, heading straight on Broadway. There was no going home. If Josie had been out to Ivan's and gone away empty-handed, she'd be looking for me again.

Giant candy canes and shiny garlanded Christmas trees clung to streetlamps, shaking in the wind. Ivan was dead, and I'd have to look elsewhere for whatever answers he might have given me. I lit another cigarette and listened to the truck's wheels humming on the slick street. By the time I'd burned halfway through the smoke, I'd passed the Catholic hospital and wheeled into the parking lot of Clayton Bennett's office.

It was a sad little structure, the wrong scale for this neighborhood of used car lots and cheap motels. I remembered several incarnations of the small brown building. It had been a fly-fishing outfitter's, a convenience store, a pawnshop. I peered out through the side window at the painted wooden plank nailed over the front door. BIG SKY ADVENTURES. Biplanes rose at each end of the sign, their tails spewing neat lines.

I tried the front door first, thinking I might luck out. On one of my first repos I spent fifteen minutes trying to slim-jim into a car before I realized it wasn't locked to begin with. But I wasn't so fortunate with Bennett's door. Skirting around to the back of the building, I tried the low windows. No luck. The back door was locked too, but I spotted a wooden cellar hatch next to the stairs. The hatch was padlocked, but the hasp was rusted and the screws holding it in place were loose. I slid my knife from my back pocket and whittled at the wood, prying the screws free, tossing the hasp aside.

The hatch opened easily, revealing the first few steps of a stairwell and darkness beyond. Leaving the entrance, I trudged back to the truck, found a flashlight, returned the way I'd come, and started down. As damp as it was, the cellar felt colder than the outside air. The beam of my flashlight swept over a rough concrete floor, walls streaked with mold and seepage. I could smell wet lime and fungus.

At the bottom of the steps I stopped and surveyed the low-ceilinged basement. Detritus from the building's former lives took up one side of the room: a cardboard cutout of a man fishing, a trout caught in midair at the end of his line, rainbow scales glistening with river water. An old poster for

Camel cigarettes, swollen-nosed Joe Camel in a motorcycle jacket. Broken neon signs. A pile of rusting chains.

In the opposite corner of the basement someone had erected a makeshift room with two particleboard walls and a flimsy door. The door sat slightly ajar. I trained my flashlight into the partitioned room and stepped inside. My head clipped a thin chain that hung down to about eye level and set it swinging. I reached up and pulled, hoping for light, but nothing happened.

At first glance, the room looked like a combination storage space and office, though why anyone would have wanted an office down here seemed unfathomable. Wire shelves bolted into the concrete side walls held enough outdoor gear to mount a small expedition to Everest: a sleeping bag; yards and yards of climbing rope; buckles and snaps; a camp stove, a tent and silvery space-age packets of dehydrated food; an arctic-weight parka. A walnut gun case sat next to the far outer wall. Through the glass doors I could see four rifles, a couple of shotguns, and several cans of pepper spray. They were the big canisters, the ones you use to fend off grizzlies and bobcats and other predators. It was easy to see why Bennett had defaulted on the Cherokee. I slid the parka on over my own coat. It alone must have been worth more than a grand.

On the other edge of the room my flashlight found a long slanted drafting table and two tall metal filing cabinets. The top of the table was piled with papers. I stepped closer, let my beam play out, and recognized maps like the ones that had spilled from Bennett's briefcase onto the snow. Flipping through them was like playing one of those which-drawing-is-different games from preschool. Each map was the same size and shape, the same colors of light green and black and red. Some were replicas. Others showed slight variations and, on close inspection, were of different plots of land. I ran my light across the words on the white border of one of the maps: UNITED STATES GROUND SURVEY.

They were government quad maps. Anyone who ventures more than a mile or two into the back-country uses them. Each map covers a remarkably small area of land, fifteen minutes' latitude by fifteen minutes' longitude. The value of their limited scope is that quad maps are highly detailed, literally showing each rock, each dip in the trail. Kristof and I had used them this past summer when we backpacked into Grasshopper Glacier down in the Absaroka Beartooth Wilderness. I moved to the filing cabinet and found more USGS maps. They were labeled with minutes and seconds instead of words, but I picked out a few familiar landmarks amid the sea of topographical lines: Bass Lake, Kootenai Creek, the Lochsa River. They all were nestled in the Selway-Bitterroot Wilderness Area, in the wild miles of land south of Missoula, near the Idaho border. I thought about Jan Jorgenson's story, how Bennett's plane had gone down there all those years ago in the Bitterroots.

The cabinets held similar maps, packed tightly into files. Each filing tab was meticulously dated, some going back as far as twenty-five years. Most were for warm-weather months, summer and early fall. The map dates for the first two decades were widely spaced, skipping two or three years at a time. Then, in the last five years, they grew closer together. The past summer was thick with maps; almost every day was dated. And then suddenly, in mid-October, the files stopped.

The maps weren't strange in themselves. Bennett was in the business of excursions, and they could have been records of flyovers he had made for Big Sky Adventures. But the chronology was odd. And something else was strange: A different section of each map was shaded with pink highlighter ink. Bennett's system was intensely methodical. Only when every inch of a particular quad had been fully shaded did he move on to a new one.

There was no doubt about it: Bennett was looking for something. Nobody combs an area of land like that for kicks.

I shone my light on the stockpile of outdoor equipment again. There was one of everything – one parka, one sleeping bag, one pair of snow-shoes. Only enough for one person. Was he trying to find the old plane? Was that what Josie and Ivan were looking for too? If it had been a training jet, as Flip and Jorgenson had said, it hardly seemed worth the effort.

The basement was like a meat locker. I closed the last filing drawer and realized I was shivering even in the parka. My cheeks were raw and frost-stung. I had taken my gloves off. I forced my numb fingers back inside and took one last look around, scanning the walls with the flashlight.

Leaving the little room behind, I followed a wooden staircase up out of the dark basement. It was freezing in the upper portion of the house as well. The whole place sparkled under a crust of frost. What moisture the air held had been crystallized. Ice motes shimmered and twinkled in the dull rectangles of light from the windows. I tried the nearest light switch, toggling it up and down. The electricity had been turned off.

It was strange, this place Bennett had left behind without knowing he would never come back. There was a wrecked feeling to the building. A half-empty coffee cup on a desk. A clock stopped at an odd hour. Houseplants wilted under the strength of the frost. It was like diving through a drowned ship, the chaos of its sinking preserved beneath layers of sea scum and coral. I had a distinct sense of trespassing, of being human and out of my element. If a sour-faced grouper had swum by or the supple body of a hammerhead shark had appeared in the doorway, I would not have been surprised. My boots left smeared footprints in the sheath of ice that coated the carpet.

I wandered through the back of the building, through the rooms Bennett had lived in. It was voyeuristic, really, witnessing the details of his life. In his bedroom, clothes were haphazardly thrown on the floor. A razor sat on the edge of the bathroom sink, a can of Barbasol. A small utilitarian kitchen was sparsely furnished with a coffeemaker, a microwave, a card table, and folding chairs.

I moved down the hallway toward the front of the house and Bennett's work space. Aerial photographs lined the walls. I recognized familiar Montana back-country: the rock cliffs of the Chinese Wall in the Bob Marshall Wilderness, Tower Falls in Yellowstone, the natural dam that marked the Mission Mountains. Black-and-white pictures showed more exotic locales: a kidney-shaped island bordered by an endless beach, a quilt of cultivated land thick with sugarcane, lush hills rising from the ocean.

The front room held a few chairs and two desks, one of which, judging by the plethora of nail polish bottles scattered along its top, must have belonged to Bennett's secretary. There was a plastic card holder at the edge of the blotter with a stack of Bennett's business cards tucked into it. Next to the holder was another stack of business cards, pink ones. I pulled the top one off the pile.

GLORIA O'KEEFE, AESTHETIC CONSULTANT, silver letters on the pink background read. Two silver roses sat on either side of the name, their stems twisting and curling. At the bottom of the card, in smaller print, was a telephone number and an address: 901 South Easy Street. Aesthetic consultant, I thought, baffled. I had to read the words several times before I realized it was just a fancy way to say beautician. I slipped the secretary's card into my pocket and moved on to the other desk, Bennett's.

He wasn't exactly a neat freak. Letters were piled on the desktop, bills in various stages of delinquency, including the Cherokee payment notice from GMAC. A Montana Power shut-off notice saying the electricity would be cut on December 20 explained the lack of heat and electricity.

In the middle of the desk was a single envelope addressed to Bennett, its top slit raggedly open. Sliding my gloves off, I fumbled with the envelope and pulled out a slick, brightly colored flyer. A man smiled up at me, his teeth a dazzling white, his cheeks airbrushed in a vain attempt to erase his wrinkles. Behind him, softly out of focus, an American flag waved in an imagined breeze. HARVEY ECKERS, the front of the flyer read, A MAN OF INTEGRITY, A MAN OF VISION. Inside the flyer was a pledge card, little black boxes indicating a range of financial possibilities – $100: contributor; $250: supporter; $1,000: partner.

Obviously Bennett hadn't thought much of Eckers's politics. Someone – I assumed it was Bennett – had taken a black marker, drawn a handlebar mustache on Eckers's upper lip, blacked out his two front teeth, and adorned his balding head with stubby horns. I felt a sudden rush of warm feeling for Bennett.

There really wasn't much of interest in the office. If I had expected some Perry Mason piece of evidence, I certainly hadn't found it. I looked out the front windows at the traffic slowly gliding by on Broadway. Across the street I could see the convenience store where Tina and Elton had supposedly gone for more malt liquor. VACANCY blinked in green neon beneath the sign for the Super Six Motel.

I ground my butt out on the frosty carpet with the heel of my boot and took one last look around the office.

*

Out in the parking lot, I cranked the engine of my Ford. The heater blew cold air into the cab. I looped around and pulled to a stop on the edge of Broadway, watching the traffic glide by. The doors of the convenience store across the street swung open and a man stumbled out, a twelve-pack cradled in his right arm. He staggered forward and lurched out into the glare of the streetlamps, dodging cars and trucks, cursing drivers as they swerved around him on the ice.

There was a scab on his right cheek and his nose was bulbous and misshapen like a cauliflower, purple as if bruised. He reached my side of the street safely, pitched across the parking lot of the Super Six Motel, and pushed his way inside one of the ground-floor rooms. Though he made me think of Tina and Elton, more than anything else he brought me back into the murky haze of my childhood memories, to another snapshot of my parents, another Fourth of July.

We were driving home late at night and I was in the back trying to stay awake, trying to keep a grip on the day that had just passed. Around us there was inky darkness, the matte black of Montana at night. Our headlights formed a tunnel, a moving stage of revelation. Tree trunks whipped by, small eyes like coals or mirrors. It was a bad road, winding and full of deer. It cut right through the heart of the reservation. Every so often my mother gasped and grabbed the dashboard; my father swerved. Another close call. Haunches flashed in front of us, antlers like maple trees in winter. Black hooves clattered like the toe shoes of ballet dancers on a wooden stage. My mother exhaled.

I fell asleep briefly, shook myself back to waking. 'Christ,' I heard my mother say. We swerved again.

I peered over the seat and saw that it was not a deer this time but a man. He careened onto the road, into the glare of the lights, then darted back out of our view. He was only visible for a split second but I saw him in his entirety: T-shirt, jeans, red Converse sneakers, baseball hat.

'Another drunken Indian,' my mother remarked. She slid a cigarette from her pack on the dashboard and struck a match, cupped her hands around the flame. The light from the match was harsh and sulfurous. I could see fine cracks around her mouth when she inhaled.

'It's the powwow tonight,' my father said.

We drove on and men kept appearing, a dozen of them maybe, their faces like pale flowers, like moths. Like the magpies that dip across the highway at dusk, daring us to travel this road.

# Eleven

I knew what a bad idea it was to go back to my house, but the maps Ivan had taken from Bennett's Jeep were there and I wanted them, needed to see how they compared to the quad maps in Bennett's office. Sliding Mrs. Carter's twenty-two from my pocket, I laid it on the seat next to me and wheeled out of the Big Sky Adventures parking lot. It was a short ride from Bennett's office to my place. Ten minutes, tops. I barreled across the bridge and straight down Higgins, easing up on the accelerator as soon as the Dairy Queen came into view. Slowing to a crawl, I craned my head toward the side window and peered down my street.

Most of my neighbors were settled in for the night. I recognized the familiar cars lined up against both curbs. The Delaneys' maroon Explorer. Mrs. Jenkins's blue Taurus. The tan mini-van that belonged to the couple on the other side of me. There was a black rectangle in front of my house, a snowless square of asphalt where I usually parked my truck. Nothing out of the ordinary.

At the next street I rounded the block, working toward my house from the west. And then I saw a blue Malibu parked just around the corner, its exhaust pipe coughing smoke into the cold air, its taillights glinting like two predatory eyes. A Subaru turned down the street toward me, shining its headlights into the blue Chevy, casting a silhouette of Josie's head from behind, her broad shoulders. I hit the gas and rolled on by without stopping.

A thousand good reasons told me to stay as far away from Kristof as possible. Josie was just one of them, the threats she'd made. All the same, I wheeled down off the Van Buren Street bridge and parked across Front Street from Kristof's apartment, my mind working on a thousand and one excuses for being there. I told myself he had a right to know about Josie, that she'd seen him at my place. It was true: I owed him that much and more. But the reality was that I wanted to see him. Besides, I had nowhere else to go.

I got out of the Ford, crossed the street, let myself into the foyer of Kristof's building, and climbed the interior stairs. Music was playing inside his apartment, something foreign and slightly jazzy. I knocked softly, heard feet shuffle across the floor. The door opened and he looked out at me, then stepped aside and motioned for me to come in.

'Where have you been?'

I shrugged. 'Working.'

'I went by your house and waited.'

I winced, thinking of him standing outside in the cold. 'Sorry.'

'I was worried,' he said, turning away from me and into the small kitchen. 'I've been calling.'

I unbuttoned the parka and kicked my boots off,

not knowing what to say. When I laid my coat on the chair by the door, Mrs. Carter's twenty-two knocked against the wood.

Kristof came back into the living room and handed me a glass of red wine. 'Jesus!' he gasped, noticing my face. 'What happened?'

I put my hand to my head, felt the scab. 'It looks worse than it is,' I told him.

He must not have had a chance to get cleaned up after work. There was a tiny constellation of blood sprayed across his forehead, a half-dozen small red flecks. His cheeks were windburned, and I could see the purple threads of veins in his skin. As close as we were to each other I could smell the stockyards on him: dusty hides and bile and excrement, the last incarnations of the animal body before death.

'What's going on, Meg?' he asked finally.

I took a sip of the wine and then another, wondering how to answer his question. I knew I should tell him, knew I should give him some little morsel of my life, at least let him know about Josie. But each reply I thought of was like the entrance to a maze, or like those whirling holes in space they always encounter in science-fiction movies. The thought of so much disclosure scared me, the maelstrom of it.

'I shouldn't be here,' I told him, setting my wine down, moving to put my boots back on. 'It's dangerous . . . for you.'

'No,' he said. I knew he hadn't understood, and yet I made no move to explain. He went to the door and turned the deadbolt. 'Please stay.'

*

When I first met Kristof, I asked him how he escaped to the West. I expected descriptions of a dark night crossing in a hot-air balloon or a mad dash across a bomb-strewn border with machine guns spitting in the distance. So when he looked over at me and said simply, 'I walked,' I was disappointed at first.

'You walked?' I asked.

He nodded.

Of course the truth, once I managed to wring it from him, was seductive just because of its simplicity. On a hot June day, Kristof walked from Yugoslavia into Greece. He was on vacation with his family and they were hiking together in the mountains and he got ahead of the group. He stood on a small outcropping of rock and watched them down in the valley below. They had stopped for lunch and he could see his mother setting out the food. His father pulled a blue-and-white tablecloth from his knapsack and snapped it open, unfurling it like a flag across the brushy ground. His brother kneeled, a tiny figure against the brown basin of the valley, and set to work cutting something – cheese, perhaps, or a loaf of bread.

Kristof reached into his pocket and pulled out a bag of loose tobacco. He rolled himself a crude cigarette and sat down on a rock to smoke. When he finished the cigarette, he took a few sips of water from the mouth of his Russian army canteen. Then, without even glancing toward the three figures below, he stood up and headed in the direction of where he thought the border might be.

I like to think of Kristof this way. I like to

imagine his father, hours later, looking at his watch, deciding it was time to head back. Or his mother, wrapping the extra portions of sausage and cheese, folding the white butcher paper neatly around them, knowing her son had gone.

In the beginning I was gratified by the momentary capacity for coldness this story revealed. Only later did I realize I had been fooled. In fact, this one act of glacial selfishness had been only a fluke. But by then it was too late for me to disentangle myself.

I thought about this as I lay in Kristof's bed and listened to the hiss of water in the pipes, thought about the ruse of his story, his body like a wily trickster. He came clean and warm from the shower and lay next to me with his lips pressed up against the back of my neck, his penis soft on my leg. I took a deep breath and brought the clean smell of him into my lungs, held it there. After he fell asleep he snored quietly. There was a rhythm to the air going in and out of the bellows of his lungs, a deep resonance in his chest, as if he were some exotic and beautiful instrument, as if his entire body had opened itself to the sound.

I fell asleep and dreamed about the stockyards and the narrow chute where they hold the cattle waiting to be killed. The animals moved against one another, scraping the musty hair of their flanks against the wood planks of the pen. Their breath was moist and warm. Their sharp hooves crackled against the hay.

A long cement table held a carcass. The animal was skinless, eviscerated, its ribs spread open like two wings. The body was blue with membrane and fascia, slick and sinewy like a newly birthed calf.

When I woke from the dream and opened my eyes to the darkness of the bedroom I could feel Kristof moving beside me. He slid his hand up along my stomach, rested his palm on the bottom curve of my breast, put his mouth on the hollow of my neck, just below my ear.

'I love you, Meg,' he whispered. This was something he used to say, in the beginning, before he knew better than to expect a reply.

He laid the words out between us in the dark like an invitation and I thought, *Desire*, only this, nothing but the unfettered longings of the flesh. I rolled over and put my thighs across his hips, felt him slip inside me.

It was well before six when I woke again, my eyes snapping open to the dark room. Careful not to wake Kristof, I padded into the kitchen, mixed a mug of instant coffee, and threw it down my throat. Except for the low hum of the refrigerator and the rush of air through the heating vents, the house was still and quiet. The wind had stopped. Out in the yard the dry snow sparkled like the billowing skirt of a sequined dress. I lit a cigarette and made another cup of coffee.

I wanted to go home, get a fresh change of clothes, brush my teeth, lie down in my own bed and sleep for days. I wanted safety, a cocoon of domesticity, the things I'd envisioned those months in New Mexico. Downing the last of the coffee, I headed back into the living room, found my coat and boots, the compact shape of the twenty-two. It was a sweet gun and I was thankful to have it, but after seeing what had happened to Ivan, I knew I'd need something more substantial to guarantee my own safety.

There was a time not long ago when Montana was free from the grubby talons of the federal government. Though we fought hard to keep things as they were, we lost in the end. Montana was the last state to raise the drinking age from eighteen to twenty-one, and we only capitulated when they threatened to take away our highway funds. Even during the oil crisis, when the rest of the country slowed down to fifty-five miles an hour, we kept cruising along at eighty. Until recently, Montana cops didn't give you fines for speeding; they asked for a five-dollar 'conservation fee,' payable on the spot, in cash. And it wasn't until the passage of the Brady bill that corner drugstores were finally forced to ask people to wait a couple of days before taking home their brand-new Smith & Wessons.

You would think that as a convicted felon such laws would keep me from getting my hands on the latest Glock or Sig-Sauer. You'd be wrong. Of all the laws the federal government has shoved down our throats, the Brady bill has so far proven to be among the least effective. If it had been a Saturday morning in summer I could have driven through the leafy neighborhoods of Missoula until I found a rummage sale that had what I wanted. And if I had had half a day to spare I could have checked the firearms section in the *Missoulian* classifieds. By afternoon I could have been well enough armed to take over a small country. But I was in a hurry, so after I left Kristof's I drove down to the Catalyst espresso bar, bought the biggest, sweetest coffee drink they sold, and cruised over to Ken Hoppie's pawnshop on Woody Street.

When I saw Hoppie's dim silhouette appear behind the darkened windows of his pawnshop, my heart surged and my pulse picked up a few beats. Ken ambled through the shop, switching on lights, turning the OPEN sign around. I waited for him to unlock the front door before I climbed out of the Ford and crossed the street.

Hoppie was already behind the counter, spreading his newspaper on the glass top, when I stepped into the shop.

'Hey, Hop,' I said, 'I brought your favorite.' I walked over to the counter and set a white paper cup in front of him. 'Almond mocha latte.'

'Whipped cream?' he asked, beaming.

I nodded.

He popped the lid and peered inside the cup. His belly spilling out over the sides of his pants, he was wearing a T-shirt that said STOP ORGANIZED CRIME, FIGHT THE IRS. His black toupee was cocked about half an inch askew on his skull. He blew at the coffee, then took a measured sip.

'You seen Darwin lately?' His lips were thick with chocolate and cream.

'Had a drink with her yesterday.'

Hop looked at me jealously. He's one of the few people from my childhood that I still see. He was always the weird one, the old man of the class. His size should have made him a shoe-in for the football team, but he was a gentle kid who didn't like getting hit. He preferred choir and drama. Most of the kids never liked Hop much, and the older we got the more they disliked him. I ran into him in Charlie's when I was first back in town, and he told me I was the only person who was ever nice to him.

'Saw her the other night at Amvets,' he said. He has a funny, pinched way of talking, as if he's squeezing the words out of his huge body.

'Oh, yeah?' Hop's a regular at the drag shows. He's too shy to admit it, but we all know he's got a raging crush on Darwin.

He nodded and his hairpiece slipped back and forth. The rug is a fashion accessory for him. He only wears it part of the time, like other people wear hats or ties.

'You just come by to bring me coffee?' he asked.

I shook my head. 'I'm here to purchase some of your fine merchandise.'

'Uh-huh. Of which variety?'

'The firearms variety,' I told him. I couldn't help smiling.

Hop leaned back, shifting himself on his stool, seeming almost as pleased to be selling as I was to be buying. 'Anything particular in mind?'

'You got anything special?'

'I've got it all, baby,' he said, winking. Then he slid the newspaper off the counter and motioned to a shiny array of handguns.

When I was in New Mexico I used to dream about coming home, about the trip northward, the scrub desert slowly turning into the blue-green folds of the Rockies. I imagined perpetual evening, light shifting across hayfields, shadows of clouds like great dark ships skimming along the mountains.

People who've never been on the inside think the system is a place to get cleaned up. But when I was in New Mexico I met all sorts of addicts. It's hard to imagine the kind of shit that gets in or how it gets there. It's the women who bring it, mostly: sisters, cousins, lovers, even mothers, sometimes. I saw a sixty-year-old woman with a dozen heroin-filled condoms in the shower room one night. She squatted down like she was giving birth and pulled the little white sacks from her vagina. I asked later how she had gotten them in, and she said her daughter had carried them inside her to the visiting room. They had made the transfer under a picnic table.

It's a rare phenomenon, the junkie's love, uncomplicated respect, pure yearning. Exiles or not, we are all addicts. We each hold some sweet memory of home, like Eden, in the jumbled cells of our bodies. It is these sensations – inclination of light, consistency of air in our lungs, particular blue of water, or filigree of hayfield – that we long to repossess. The smell of hot linen fresh from the dryer. The first inhalation of wind-beaten sage. The first blaze of sunshine leaping at the cornea. Something familiar, holy.

When Hop bent down and unlocked the back of the case, when he pulled his first offer, a Sile-Benelli nine-millimeter auto, from its shelf, when he turned it over and slipped the checkered ridges of the walnut stock into the cup of my waiting palm, all I could think was that I was home.

I fingered the sight at the end of the barrel and ran my thumb along the protrusion of steel at the base of the grip.

'Chrome-lined bore,' I heard Hop say. 'Fixed barrel, locked breech.' It was like listening to someone from the other side of a fever.

I put the Sile-Benelli on the case and stepped back, scanning the other guns, each one a perfect mechanism, simple and deadly.

'Shit, what's that?' I asked, pointing to a huge revolver on the top shelf. It was the largest handgun I'd ever seen.

Hop chuckled. 'That one's a beauty, huh? Taurus Raging Bull. It's bigger than a forty-four Magnum. Makes Dirty Harry's gun look like a peashooter.'

'What's it shoot?'

'Four-fifty-four Casull.' Hop grinned.

'Not exactly practical, is it?'

'Not unless you're out to bag an elk. It's a show gun, really. I'll probably end up keeping it, just to have it around. For laughs.'

I scanned the case again, my eyes settling on a glossy auto pistol at the far end of the lower shelf. 'That one,' I said, pointing.

Hop smiled. 'Sig P two-twenty-nine. Beautiful,' he remarked. He stretched his arm out, his breath laboring, and fumbled for the stock.

Imagine sweaty nights in the back of your father's car. Imagine the cotton of a bra pushed back to reveal white skin, the rusty circle of the areola. Imagine the first boy who kissed you, the pad of his thumb against the bulb of your nipple, his tongue gliding across your teeth, the callow pressure of his hand on your waist.

I took the gun from Hop, felt the weight of it in my palm.

'Everything in working order?' I asked.

'You bet.'

'Any way to do this off the books?'

Hop took another sip of his latte. 'Goddamn Brady bill.' He sighed, shaking his head, setting his cup down.

I smiled sympathetically.

'Fuck it.' He beamed. 'We can work something out.' He readjusted his weight, sat back on his stool. I could hear him sucking his teeth.

'You got some extra magazines hanging around?'

'Shit, girl.' He whistled. 'What you planning to do here, rob a bank?'

'Just personal security.'

'Oh, yeah,' he said, tilting his head, surveying me. 'I understand.' Then he hoisted himself off his perch and waddled toward the back of the shop.

I left Hop's and headed across the river to my place, praying Josie had gotten tired of waiting and decided to give up her watch for a few hours at least. I still wanted the maps, wanted to see if they were the same section of land as the ones in Bennett's office. And I had a phone call to make. I needed to talk to Vera Popov and ask her exactly what she'd seen.

I took the back street to my house, wanting to spot the Malibu before Josie saw me. But there was no sign of her car. Tracks in the snow wheeled away from the space where she'd been parked the night before, made a U-turn.

Lucky break, I told myself, but as I rolled closer to my little cottage I felt my luck fast diminishing. There was a car parked outside the front walkway, a blue-and-white cruiser with police markings. The driver's door opened and Jeff Riley stepped out into the street, waving his hands, motioning for me to pull over.

For a second I thought I'd just keep driving; then reason got the better of me and I eased the truck to the curb.

'Hey, Riley,' I said, rolling my window down, making no move to get out. 'Or do you want me to call you Chief?'

Riley looked at me seriously. More Gary Cooper than John Wayne. 'Why don't you invite me inside, Megan?'

I didn't say anything. He stepped closer, put a gloved hand on my door, popped the latch.

The Sig was in a brown paper bag on the front seat, and I watched Riley's eyes linger on it. 'You didn't come home last night,' he remarked.

Shrugging, I climbed down out of the truck. 'After you,' I told him, following as he turned up the walk and climbed my front stairs. Stepping around him on the porch, I opened the door with my key and motioned for him to go inside.

'Make yourself at home,' I said. His cheeks were red. His body radiated cold. He stopped in the middle of the living room and looked around, his eyes taking in what was left of the mess Josie had made. The snow his boots had tracked onto the carpet was already turning to water.

'Where were you last night?' he asked, taking a handkerchief from the back pocket of his jeans, wiping his nose.

I shrugged, trying to ignore the clutter, hoping he'd think I was just a slob. 'Around. Did some scouting for Flip.'

'Whereabouts, exactly?'

'Went up to Superior. Checking in on a Lumina I've been trying to get.' Even as I said this, I knew the lie was futile. I've never had a cop ask me where I was who didn't already know the answer.

'Don't bullshit me, Meg.' Riley sat down on the couch. His legs were long and his knees drew up close to his chest. I could see the outline of a gun beneath his coat.

I stepped into the kitchen and found some cigarettes. Riley swiveled his head to the doorway, watched me come back. I sat down opposite him and struck a match, inhaled. I kept quiet, my eyes trained on Mrs. Carter's brown shag carpet.

'About six o'clock this morning one of Ivan Popov's cronies walks into the station. Big ugly guy, white as a ghost. Says he was just out in East Missoula. You know what else he says?'

I shook my head.

'He says Ivan's dead. Now, what do you know about that?'

'What a shame.'

Riley slumped forward, put his head in his

hands. 'See, here's the problem, Meg. He also says you and Ivan exchanged some not-so-friendly words recently. That you assaulted him. Says that's how you got that shiner.'

I shrugged. 'And?'

'Gimme one of those cigarettes, will ya?' Riley said.

I tossed him the pack.

'You know how many times I've quit in the last ten years?' he muttered, fumbling desperately with the packaging, his hands shaking. He stopped abruptly, threw the whole thing on the floor. 'God-damn it, Meg. You're looking better than anyone for this.'

I looked up, let what he was trying to say sink in. 'You think it was me killed him?'

'I didn't say that.' Riley twisted his wedding band, looked hungrily at the discarded pack of smokes.

'Ivan's got plenty of enemies,' I said. 'Why pin this on me?'

I could hear Riley breathing and the far-off sound of a snow shovel scraping against concrete.

'I found out what happened in New Mexico, Meg,' he said apologetically. 'Why didn't you tell me?'

I took a long pull off my cigarette. 'It didn't seem much like your business, what I got sent away for. The guy was a jerk, my part-time boyfriend. We were both drunk when it happened.'

Riley paused for a moment, twisted his ring again. 'You knifed a guy, Meg. Can't you see how bad this looks?'

'Shit,' I protested. 'It was different. I was pissed off, got caught up in the moment. Whoever did this to Ivan got a hard-on over it.'

'I'll let you know if we need you,' he said, sounding like a disappointed high school principal. Taking a deep breath, he pushed himself up off the couch. 'You never did realize I was on your side, did you?'

I sat back and watched him go. He opened the door, and the room filled with a bone-chilling cold.

'You know that Indian woman you were asking about?' he said, turning back to face me.

'Tina Red Deer?'

'Yeah, Red Deer.' He nodded. 'She a friend?'

I shrugged.

'We closed the case against her this morning.'

'What are you talking about, you closed the case?'

'She hung herself in her cell last night. Just thought you might want to know. Seemed like you had an interest.'

I stared up at him, my jaw aching as if I had just been slapped.

He adjusted his hat, stepped onto the porch, and was gone.

I listened to him leaving, his boots popping on the grainy ice of the sidewalk, a car door slamming, an engine turning over. I sat there, motionless, until my cigarette burned down and I could feel the heat of it on my knuckles. In my mind I walked through the cold corridors of the jail, through the halls that smelled of fresh paint and damp cement. It was night, the walls and ceilings that otherworldly shade of slate gray that I associate with sleepwalking. Angular slabs of moonlight fell across the floor.

It was more like a jail in the movies than the jails I had known. Cells with gray bars and bunk beds. Rats skittering past my feet. All around me women were sleeping. Bodies breathed, turned, moved their lips, muttered to themselves. It was like being in a lair, an animal place of communal hibernation.

Down the corridor a chair banged against the floor. A rope creaked. I could see a shadow kicking, feet fighting the air like a swimmer treading water. This was how she died, I thought. The cords tightening around the muscles of her neck, a gasp and maybe regret, a wish to undo the last leap. Tina Red Deer. This woman who might have been my sister.

# Twelve

With Riley gone I felt vulnerable and exposed in the empty house. There was no telling when Josie might come back to look in on me, and I didn't want to be around when she did. I checked my answering machine. There was a message from Amos Ortenson, a frantic, garbled plea to call him back, something about Room 103. I jotted down the number he had left and slipped the scrap of paper into the pocket of my pants.

Pulling a brown grocery bag from one of the kitchen drawers, I threw a change of clothes into it, some spare underwear, and a toothbrush. Bennett's briefcase was in my bedroom closet. I hauled it out and headed for the door.

I stopped at the gas station around the corner from my place and dialed Amos's number.

A woman's voice answered lazily on the second ring. 'Thunder Bird Motel.'

'One-oh-three? Amos Ortenson's room?' I asked skeptically, wondering if I'd copied the number down wrong. I couldn't imagine why Amos would have checked into the Thunder Bird.

'Hold on.'

The line clicked over. There was a dull, insistent

ringing and then the woman's voice again. 'He's not answering. Do you want to leave a message?'

'No, thanks,' I told her, still puzzled. It was strange, really, but then Amos was a strange guy.

I put him out of my mind for the time being, fished some more change from my coat pocket, and dialed the Popovs' Hot Springs number. A man picked up. When I told him I wanted to talk to Vera, I got a bored and contemptuous hello.

'Mrs. Popov?' I asked.

'*Da,*' she said lazily, as if interacting with another human being was far beneath her. I got the feeling that her use of the Russian word was based more on its compactness and effortless pronunciation than on the fact that it was part of her native language.

'How did you manage to get home this morning, without your keys?'

There was a long pause on the other end of the line. I heard Vera's hair rustle against the mouthpiece.

'Who is this?' she asked.

'I met you the other day, up in Hot Springs. I was there to see Nick. You brought us tea by the pool.'

Silence crackled on the other end of the line.

'I've got your purse, Mrs. Popov,' I continued, not sure if she remembered who I was or not. 'A little red number with gold trimmings.'

'So?' Her voice was steady, cool as a cucumber. She functioned exceptionally well in monosyllables, I thought.

'I could bring it to the house. Maybe your husband would like to know where I found it.'

'Be my guest.' I heard her strike a match, the faint crackling of dry tobacco and paper.

'Also, the chief of police was here earlier. We go way back, years. I thought he might be interested as well to know you were there.'

Vera paused again. I was impressed with her ability to wait, to measure her words. Most people open their mouths without giving any thought to what they're about to say.

'What do you want?' she asked.

'I want to know what you saw.'

'And you will return my purse?'

'Yes.'

'Good,' Vera said. She used the word differently than I would have, an indication of agreement. As in, Now that that's all settled. 'You are in Missoula?'

'Yes.'

'We will meet at the Y. At Fred's. You know it?'

'Yes, I know it.'

'Good. You ask for me. Two hours.'

Back in the cab of my truck, I opened the briefcase and thumbed through the stack of maps, checking dates and locations. Everything matched up to what I'd seen in Bennett's office. The maps were of the same area, a huge chunk of forest off the Lochsa River, near the Idaho border. I tried to visualize the land. All that came to mind was trees and more trees, hilly folds of backcountry. An X in the upper right-hand corner of one of the quads marked the Powell Ranger Station. Like the maps in Bennett's office, these were crisscrossed with pink ink. The dates were recent, from October to the beginning of December.

I lit a cigarette and studied the quads, the creek beds like thin blue veins, the fibers of the paper soaked a bright rose where Bennett had highlighted sections of land. If he was looking for a plane in there, it would seem minute as a needle in the immense haystack of the Bitterroot Mountain Range.

Peeling out of the gas station parking lot, I headed over to the Missoula Club to kill some time, got a burger and some coffee, and took the interstate out toward the windy western side of the valley. The Y was visible long before I got to it. It stood high and alone, a monument to cross-country trucking. Spindly-legged neon signs towered above the compound. Lights blinked time and temperature, gas and cigarette prices, steak and eggs for five dollars and ninety-five cents. Billboards for Fred's beckoned. All nude. Twenty-four hours.

Taking the exit, I squeezed the Ford in between a Wal-Mart semi and a livestock truck. The lot smelled of sheep shit and wet wool. Pink-and-black noses pressed against metal air holes. Red-rimmed eyes peered out, blinked. I trudged toward the front door, wishing Vera and I could have met anywhere but here.

This time of day there wasn't much doing at Fred's. I told the doorman I was there to see Vera and he waved me on, pointed to the bartender. I made my way to the bar, keeping my eyes to the ground as much as possible.

'I'm looking for Vera,' I told the bartender. He was short and stocky, his arms thick with muscles. His black hair was slicked back against his skull, lined with comb marks. In the mirror behind him I could see the stage. A young girl who looked like she had just recently given birth swung her hips lazily, dropped to her knees, looked out into the darkness. I felt like I might be sick.

The man grunted. 'This way.' He came out from behind the bar and led me down a dim corridor. 'In here,' he said. I stepped through a door marked PRIVATE DANCES, heard it close behind me.

The room I was in was tiny, a dimly lit cubicle with a single wooden chair. The top half of one wall was two-way mirrored glass. On the other side of my reflection I could barely make out the outline of another figure. A ghostly head, shoulders, the bright coal of a cigarette: someone watching me. I sat down in the chair and waited, looked at the floor, pretended not to notice my observer. The room reminded me of the worst aspects of incarceration. The lack of privacy, the almost erotic voyeurism of it all. At night in New Mexico I would lie awake and listen to the women on either side of me, the creaking of old mattresses, skin working against skin.

I heard the doorknob rattle and looked up to see Vera. She came in and closed the door behind her, leaned her back up against the wall. She was wearing leopard-skin boots with needle-thin heels, a black leather skirt, and a thick faux-leopard coat. In her right hand was a Beretta Bobcat. It was a small gun, a twenty-five caliber, and though she wasn't pointing it at me, it was menacing none-theless. I shifted in my chair and swallowed hard.

'Nice place,' I said, trying to sound unflustered. 'Good choice.'

'I used to work here. They are friendly with me,' she explained. 'This is where I met Nick.' Her English was almost flawless.

'You didn't come to America together?'

She waved her hand dismissively. 'No.'

I looked at the gun and then at our reflections in the mirror. 'You were watching me.'

Vera nodded.

'Are you thinking of shooting me?' I asked.

'No,' she said, her voice faltering a little. 'I didn't know, on the phone . . . if you were lying.' She put the gun in the pocket of her coat and pulled a pack of cigarettes out. 'I thought you might have been her.'

'Who?'

'The woman,' Vera said, a shudder working its way through her thin body. She sucked on her cigarette and stared at the red purse on my lap. 'Are you working with Ivan?'

'No.'

'Are you police?' she said, suspiciously.

I shook my head again. Though I could have easily been lying, my answer seemed to satisfy her.

'Nick says you are one hell of a classy lady. I don't see this, really.'

I shrugged, held the purse up so Vera could get a better look. 'What happened last night?'

'No police,' she said. 'You promise this?'

I could see a skin of fear on her, like a water

mark caught deep under a veneer. It was something common between us, something I understood.

'I promise,' I told her.

'Ivan has been jumpy these last few days, not himself. So when we heard the car come to the back and saw it was one we didn't know, he told me, "Vera, go to the ladies' room." ' She sighed deeply, lit a fresh cigarette off the end of her old one, flicked the butt onto the floor. 'So I went, of course. The bathrooms there, you have to go outside to get to them.' She wrinkled her nose at the thought. 'So I took my coat but not my purse. It was all a hurry, you know, quick, quick. I stayed for maybe ten minutes, but Ivan didn't come to get me and it was cold, so I went out from the bathroom.'

She stopped talking and wrapped her arms tight around her chest.

'Did you see who it was?' I asked.

'I saw her leaving, from behind,' she said, her fingers tightening around her upper arms, the rims of her nails turning white from the pressure. 'When I went inside I could smell what she had done.' Vera looked straight at me, breathing hard. 'Give me my purse,' she said.

I thought about the garage, the odors of blood and grease.

'You should tell the police,' I told her.

She leaned her head back and laughed. 'You know my husband, yes? His business?'

'Yes.'

'Then you know why we cannot involve ourselves with the police.'

I held the red bag out to her, then snatched it

away. 'What about Ivan's business? What was he doing with Clayton Bennett?'

'There was an old plane. Ivan's treasure hunt.' Vera spat the words out contemptuously. 'They were like two little boys.'

She reached greedily for the bag. I let her take it. 'Just the plane?'

'He didn't talk business with me.' She smoothed her skirt across her thighs. 'I hope you find whoever did this.' She looked straight at me and her eyes were dark and wet. 'I hope you kill her.' Putting her hand on the doorknob, she disappeared into the hallway.

Try as I might, I couldn't get Amos Ortenson or his new residence out of my mind. Troubling as a hangnail, he'd been lurking in my psyche during my meeting with Vera. I thought of him the whole way back into town, and when I hit the Van Buren Street exit I headed down off the interstate and east toward Hellgate Canyon and the Thunder Bird Motel. The wind was strong on this side of the valley. My old Ford shuddered and swerved past the Eastgate Lounge.

A premature dusk darkened the sky, and a few stray clouds, their bellies reflecting the orange lights of the city, skidded across the valley. Fluorescent light spilled out of the twenty-four-hour grocery store, illuminating a pile of bedraggled Christmas trees. Formless in his layers of clothes, a derelict paced in front of the automatic doors.

At the far end of the lot, its cinder-block back to the wind, name blazing in twenty feet of red neon, sat the Thunder Bird Motel. A giant train of toys was strung in lights and plastic garlands over the windows of the office. Teddy bears and happy soldiers waved from their boxcars. I pulled into a spot at the side of the building closest to the river, near the Dumpsters, and cut the engine. Out the window of the Ford I could see the Clark Fork, white ice crossed with black spider veins of water.

Squinting against the lurid purple breezeway lighting, I counted down the first-floor rooms. My eyes stopped at 103, and I climbed out of the Ford and headed across the parking lot. I had a nasty feeling about this whole thing with Amos. I raised my hand to knock on the door, then hesitated a moment and slid the Sig from the back of my pants.

I knocked once, got no answer from inside.

'Amos,' I called, putting my lips right up next to the wood, 'it's Meg.'

I tried the knob, felt it give in my hand. The door swung open.

'Amos,' I tried again, pivoting around the door-jamb, once again getting no answer.

I had heard the Thunder Bird had a honeymoon suite, and evidently 103 was it. Most of the furnishings were shades of red or pink, decorated with plump hearts. A heart-shaped satin headboard, quilted, with black studs, was clamped to the wall above the mammoth king-sized bed. The ceiling was covered in mirrors. There was no sign of Amos.

I kicked the door closed behind me, reached back, and flipped the lock. From what I could see, Room 103 wasn't actually a suite. It was just the one room with a bathroom jutting off it in the back. Soggy footprints crossed the red shag from the hot tub to the bathroom and I followed them. Stepping over a pile of clothes, I recognized Amos's torn jeans, his Sex Pistols T-shirt. Though muted, the television was on, tuned to some holiday pornography. It was tasteful programming: Mrs. Claus bent over a stack of presents, getting banged from behind by an elf.

The room was freezing, and when I stepped into the bathroom I saw why. The window over the toilet was open as far as it would go. Putting my hands on the sill, I peered out into the wind. The snow was muddled with confused footprints, indentations where it looked like someone fell or was dragged. And there, at the edge of the encroaching knapweed, two sharp points of hair, one red, one green, the festive colors of Amos's Mohawk.

Turning from the window, I sprinted through the heart-filled room, down the breezeway, and around the Dumpsters to the back of the Thunder Bird.

Let me say this: I'm not unfamiliar with the various aspects of death and human destruction. But what I saw in the snow-ghosted brush was something for which I was completely unprepared. All six feet of Amos Ortenson lay chest up, naked in the snow. Except for the glossy trickle of blood at the corner of his mouth, his face was undisturbed. It was his body that had been pillaged. Someone had taken a knife to his chest and belly and split the skin as a hunter might split the tough hide of a deer. One neat cut, long and deep, ran from the base of his rib cage to the bowl of his pelvis. At the bottom of the gash, his genitals were still intact.

He hadn't been dead for long. His blood in the snow was the consistency of thick chocolate syrup. Even in the sub-zero cold I could smell him, the rich mineral odor of the interior of his body. Retching, kicking snow over my tracks, I put my hand to my mouth and backed away.

In anticipation of the holiday shoppers, they had turned the outdoor speakers on at the twenty-four-hour grocery store. Nat King Cole's voice roved, tinny and hollow, across the empty parking lot. I stepped up into the Ford, cranked the heater, and tried to envision roasting chestnuts, Yuletide fires, anything besides Amos's pale carcass. *Merry Christmas*, Cole warbled. I shifted into drive and pulled away from the Thunder Bird.

# Thirteen

As I rolled onto Broadway and headed west, there was only one thought in my mind: to be among others. It hardly mattered who they were; most anyone with a pulse would have done. What I really wanted was to slide into bed with Kristof, to take my clothes off and feel the communion of his skin against my own. I wanted to watch him sleep, watch each breath move in and out of his body. Or maybe run my hand down his spine, toward the cradle of his pelvis, the flat plane at the base of his back, the two symmetrical eyes where the muscles connect. Like a butterfly, I've often thought, a great butterfly encircling him.

I was only a few blocks from his place but I fought off the urge to be with him. I had other things to worry about. Besides, Amos's and Ivan's deaths had brought out strange, reckless feelings in me and I didn't want to say anything I might regret later. Instead, I cruised over to the one place where I knew I wouldn't feel lonely. The sun had just gone down when I pulled into a spot by the back door of the Oxford Saloon. It was happy hour at other bars around town, but here, where the atmosphere tends toward perpetual gloom, there were only a few stragglers in the café and some diligent gamblers back in the flickering light of the poker and keno machines.

I found a stool at the counter and ordered a cup of coffee.

'You eating?' the waitress asked. She looked relieved when I shook my head no.

I watched her trundle down to the far end of the counter and return to her copy of *People* magazine.

The coffee was strong and bitter, the dregs of a pot that undoubtedly had been cooking away since that morning. But it was hot and I was bone-cold and happy to have it. I lit a cigarette and looked up at the back-lit menu board above the grill. BRAINS AND EGGS, the sign read, and then, in parentheses, BECAUSE HE NEEDS 'EM.

That was Amos's problem, I thought, still trying to block the image of his torn body from my mind. Some extra smarts might have kept him alive. But this time I wondered if it was not a *lack* of knowledge that got him into trouble but *too much*. He might have known more about Bennett's death than he was letting on.

A coffee-stained *Missoulian* lay on the counter. I picked it up and flipped aimlessly through the pages, trying to keep myself occupied. My daily horoscope looked strangely good. No mention of violent death. *Take a risk with romance!* it counseled.

Putting the local section aside, I glanced at the front page. A small head shot in an article along the bottom caught my eye. It was Harvey Eckers, the idiot billionaire. The photo beside him showed his opponent, Gregory Jacobs, his mouth open in a dazzling smile. POLLS SHOW ECKERS SLIPPING, the headline read. I thought of the picture in Bennett's office, the horns sprouting from the candidate's head.

It seemed Jacobs had found a way to counter the accusations of infidelity Eckers had made against him. According to the paper, Eckers's uncle, Kingston Starre, a former U.S. senator, had been heavily involved in the anticommunist movement in the fifties. Starre had been in charge of sniffing out what he called 'leftist sympathizers' in the military. None of this was news, but Eckers had been in the Air Force at the time, and Jacobs's camp was hinting that Eckers had worked for his uncle.

I finished the article and put the paper aside. With no real mud to sling, Jacobs was grasping at straws. Once the initial squall blew over, Eckers would unlikely be any worse for the wear. Though voters might care about a politician's inability to keep his pants on, I doubted the dry history of American politics could hold their attention. Fishing my wallet out of my pocket, I thumbed through the billfold, slapped five dollars on the counter, and waved the waitress over for some change. She took my money and counted out four ones.

'They're all the same,' she remarked, looking down at the Eckers headline, shaking her head. The crow's-feet around her eyes were caked with pink concealer, the makeup just a few shades too dark for her skin.

I left her a dollar and stuffed the rest of my

change back in my wallet. My billfold was crammed with junk: gas station receipts, business cards, scraps of paper with old phone numbers. The corner of a pink card stuck up from between two ten-dollar bills. Sliding the card out, I forced the wallet closed.

'Aesthetician,' I said to myself, scanning the name of Clay Bennett's secretary. The East Missoula address read South Easy Street. I glanced down at the paper one last time, at Harvey Eckers's face in black-and-white, then headed out the door and east again toward Hellgate Canyon.

As might be expected, Easy Street bore little resemblance to its name. It turned out to be a cul-de-sac of bland one-story homes deep in the darkness of the canyon. Broken tricycles poked out from wind-glazed snowdrifts. Castaway appliances, rusted washers and dryers and electric ranges, dotted the front yards. Random houses displayed a few halfhearted attempts at Christmas kitsch, here a flashing line of color, there a troop of reindeer climbing the eaves.

I coasted until I found Gloria's house, cut the engine, and climbed out of the truck. The lights in front were on, and a squat tree glistened in the picture window. I made my way up the icy steps and knocked. A dog barked viciously on the other side of the door, its claws rasping across the wood. I knocked again and stepped back.

'Christ, Glo! Get the goddamn door, will ya?' It was a man's voice, muffled by the blare of a television.

Several moments passed, punctuated by the hell-hound within. Finally the door swung open, revealing a neat little woman in powder-puff-pink slippers and a lime-green jogging suit. Her hair was dyed a gruesome shade of eggplant, gray at the roots. A long thin cigarette poked out from between her lips. She had the dog, a small Jack Russell terrier, by the collar and was holding his scrabbling front paws off the floor.

'Can I help you?' She looked up at me, talking around the filter of the cigarette.

'Mrs. O'Keefe?' I held the pink business card out to her, as if in explanation of my visit.

'Ms.,' she corrected, then turned to the man whose voice I had heard. 'Hey, dickhead. Put the fucking beast down in the basement, will ya?' Her voice and language were so far removed from her appearance that she almost seemed possessed. I moved back, expecting her head to start spinning at any moment.

Dickhead leaned back into the soft vinyl of his La-Z-Boy and hooked his fingers around his neck. There was some kind of Christmas variety show on the TV, and he kept his eyes glued to it.

'I'm talkin' to you,' Gloria barked, getting zero response. She turned back to me and lifted the cigarette from her mouth with her free hand, her voice switching to sugary sweet. 'I'll be right back, honey. Come on in.' She disappeared and I heard a door open and slam shut, then the sound of distant howls.

Closing the front door behind me, I took a step into the living room. 'What ya watching?' I asked, trying to break the uncomfortable silence with Dickhead. He shifted his weight and grunted, his T-shirt riding up over the exposed flab of his belly.

Gloria reappeared in the doorway, threw him the evil eye. 'My studio's back this way, honey.' She beamed at me, motioning for me to follow her.

We crossed through the kitchen and passed into a spare room in the back of the house. Gloria flicked an overhead lamp on, revealing a beautician's chair and a long vanity with a mirror.

'You sure look like you need help,' she said, then added, 'No offense.'

'Actually, Ms. O'Keefe—'

'Gloria.'

'Actually, Gloria, I didn't come for a beauty consult.'

'Oh.' She stubbed her cigarette out hurriedly and pulled the top of her jogging suit tight around her, looking somewhat hurt.

'I'm with the Montana Backcountry Pilots Association,' I told her. It was a lame lie, but it was the only thing I could come up with.

'We already give money to the Shriners,' she said warily.

I shook my head. 'I'm not here for money. I understand you worked for Clayton Bennett.'

Gloria nodded.

'He was a member of our club. We're doing a memorial edition of our newsletter. I was wondering if I could ask you some questions.'

Gloria looked at me skeptically, her mouth gone slack. 'What was the name of your club?'

'Montana Backcountry Pilots Association,' I

said, hoping I gave the same name the second time around.

'Never heard of it.'

I forced the biggest, corniest smile I could muster. 'Clay's been a member in good standing for almost a decade now.'

She backed away from me and propped her thighs on the vanity, still skeptical.

I looked at my watch and scowled at my reflection in the mirror, touched my cheek. The last thing I wanted was a makeover, but I needed to get her talking.

Gloria pulled another Virginia Slim out of the pocket of her warm-up suit and fingered her lighter. 'Autumn,' she remarked, taking my bait. Her eyes narrowed in on my face.

'Excuse me?'

'Definitely an autumn. It's your color scheme.' Tossing the cigarette on the vanity, she reached her hand out and lifted my chin. 'I could do something about that shiner. A complimentary consultation.'

I looked at myself again, feigned great interest. 'What the heck,' I said. 'Let's do it!'

Gloria smiled and motioned me to her chair. 'Don't worry,' she said, coming around behind me, gazing at my face in the mirror. 'We'll go with a real natural look this first time. No one'll even know you're wearing makeup. It's all about freshness this season.'

I nodded and tried to keep from grimacing. She went over to the vanity and picked through her selection of jars and compacts.

'So, about Clay. We want to focus on his love of

mountaineering. I understand he had a real affinity with the Bitterroots, spent a lot of time up there.'

Gloria laughed. 'Cut the shit, honey. Did you ever actually meet Clay?' She bent over me and touched a small wet foundation sponge to my face.

'Is it that obvious?'

She winked, continued dabbing at my face.

'I just pick up some spare cash writing for this newsletter. To tell you the truth, I've never even been in one of those little planes. But I really would appreciate anything you can tell me.' I tried my cornball smile again. Miraculously, it seemed to work.

Gloria stepped back and surveyed the progress she had made on my face. She picked up the discarded Virginia Slim and lit it. 'First off,' she started, 'there wasn't any affinity with the Bitterroots. Clay hated those goddamned mountains. If he'd had his way about it he never would have even looked at them again.'

There was a muffled cry for service from the living room. Gloria opened the door and stuck her head out. 'Go to hell!' she screamed, and ducked back inside. 'You ever been married?' she asked.

I shook my head.

'Good. It's a crock of shit they try to sell you on.' She put her cigarette down and picked up a little brush. 'Eyes closed, please.' Bristles fanned across my lids. 'You don't know Clay's story?'

'Not very much of it, anyway.' I looked at her. I wanted to hear her version of Bennett's life.

'It's amazing, really.' She looked at me pointedly. 'Romantic, if you ask me. He was an officer in the

Air Force Reserves, back in the fifties. A jet pilot. Anyway, he dropped a plane down in the Bitterroots.'

'He crashed, you mean?'

'What else would I mean, honey? Early spring, but you know how that kind of weather can be. Worse than this, sometimes. Can you imagine?'

I shook my head and glanced out the window at the menace of winter. No lie here. I truly could not imagine. 'How'd he survive?'

'Look down, please.' She touched a pencil to my upper lid. 'He found a fire lookout. There was a cupboard full of canned beans and enough books to keep him going till the snow melted.'

'He read?'

Gloria laughed again. It was a throaty laugh, truthful. 'Shit, no. Those books were the only dry fuel he could find. He burned 'em to keep warm. He was there for two months. When he walked out they had already declared him dead. He scared the shit out of the two fishermen who found him, probably looked like a corpse. Imagine that, looking at your own death certificate. Look up, please.'

'But he made it?'

'Sure. He was a hero. Of course, I was very young at the time.' She touched her breast briefly, as if to emphasize her former youth. 'You can look, but I'm not quite finished.'

Gloria's hands left my face, and I opened my eyes to stare at the bizarre creature in the mirror. I looked like Tammy Faye Bakker on a bad day. 'I heard they never found the plane?'

'Clay always said it was on account of the

weather, that storm. He said everything got covered up by the snow. They gave up eventually, but not Clay.' She shook her head and wiped at her eyes. A bright tear lingered on her cheek. I thought of Dickhead in the living room and wondered if Bennett was more than just Gloria's boss. 'You know, he'd been looking for that plane ever since.'

I climbed out of the chair, trying to avoid the reflection of my face. 'You said Clay was a reserve pilot, right?'

Gloria nodded.

'What did he do? For work, I mean.'

'I don't know exactly. I guess he flew for that fruit company some.'

'What fruit company?'

'Let's see if I can remember. Starry Fruit. Star Fruit. Something like that. Out in eastern Washington. Clay lived in Spokane before he moved here.' She put her finger to her lower lip, knit her eyebrows together.

'He dust crops for them?'

'No idea,' she said, relaxing her brow. 'They still paid him, though.'

'Like a pension?'

'I guess, though it wasn't regular. More like every year or so he'd get a check.'

'A lot of money?' I asked, instantly regretting the question, wondering if I'd gone too far.

Gloria cocked her head and looked at me sideways. 'Enough,' she said.

The short stretch of Highway 200 leading out of the canyon was wind-burnished, slick. The city had the big de-icing machine out, and the hulking truck crawled along in front of me, spraying jets of steaming chemicals onto the asphalt. Dusted with the exhaust of cars and the soft sifting of fallout from the paper mill, the snow had turned from luminous white to drab gray. Caked drifts, striated with sand and ice, lined the road.

I drove aimlessly, trying to piece my thoughts together and decide what to do next. Downtown was crowded with frantic last-minute shoppers. The windows of the big brick department store housed blinking Christmas trees, bands of mechanical carolers, disembodied hearths with tissue-paper fires crackling in their grates. As I pulled up to a red light on Front Street, my truck momentarily lost its grip on the road and I came two inches from slamming into a package-heavy pedestrian. The woman glared out from above the coils of her red and green scarf and raised her free hand, showing me her middle finger. The light turned green and I was off, whistling past the fluttering hem of her coat.

There was something more to Bennett's search than just the old plane. That much was certain. Had he been carrying something that day all those years ago, something worth his life – and Ivan's and Amos's too? Ivan's treasure hunt, Vera had said. What kind of treasure could possibly be in the forty-year-old wreckage of an Air Force jet?

I crossed the Higgins Avenue bridge and drove south. At the Dairy Queen I slowed and looked down the street toward my house. Two cars sat at the curb, two black-and-white vultures with their unmistakable racks of lights. Riley, I thought. The doughnut eaters.

It's funny how easily your perspective can change. I never really wanted the house, the responsibility of it, the cascade of leaves in the fall that required raking, the rambling grass that constantly needed to be mowed. I dreaded August, the vigilance it required, the panicked switching of the sprinklers. When I first moved in I hadn't realized what I'd gotten myself into. I thought I could get by with minimal effort, but at the first sign of sun-browned grass the neighbors were over, Mrs. Jenkins or the Delaneys from across the street. They barraged me with friendly tips. 'The leaf truck's coming around this week,' they would mention casually when they met me on the street. Or, 'Do you need some help starting your mower? My boy'd be glad to look at it for you.'

Being a good neighbor is all about keeping up appearances. It doesn't matter what you do behind your door. It doesn't matter that Mrs. Perkins in the yellow house starts drinking cheap Chablis when her husband leaves for work at eight o'clock in the morning, or that the man in the phony brick Tudor likes to sneak into his daughter's room at night and watch her sleep.

So I always did my part and secretly wished for the old, untethered freedom. But when I saw the two cruisers snugged up against my curb, everything changed. For a moment I wanted inside. I wanted the refuge of domesticity, the harbor of four walls. I had to catch myself, the way you violently shake yourself from that first moment of slumber. Let them have it, I said, not turning. I reached down and touched the butt of my Sig, as if it were a talisman, a shiny penny in my pocket.

# Fourteen

Speaking strictly in terms of topography you'd have to say Montana is two states, one honest, the other deceitful. Out east, where the Rocky Mountain Front breaks into the grasslands of the Northern Plains, nothing is hidden. The geological history of the earth is laid out in plain sight, the great floods and upheavals, the apocalypse of ice and snow that carved the continent. Even in the western mountains, valleys are treeless, wide and long, and evidence abounds of the scrape and creak of prehistoric forces that shaped the land.

It's not until you head out of Missoula and toward Idaho that the deception begins. Here, the mountains rise around you, breaking your view, and it's easy to forget the creased miles of impenetrable land, the untold acres of the Nine Mile Divide, the tangled peaks of the Bitterroot Range. Huddled around the highway, civilization seems more extensive, its grasp less tenuous than it actually is.

Looking back on that evening, I might say the direction I chose had something to do with the illusion of order. I wanted to disappear, to be as invisible as the wild interior of Montana lurking behind the pine-stubbled hills. Or I might say there was a question I still wanted answered.

Leaving my house and Missoula behind, I followed the twisting bed of the Clark Fork through Alberton and Tarkio and Superior. The blacktop was glazed with the cold breath of the river and I took the turns slowly, holding my breath at each bend in the road, imagining myself careening through the guardrails and down into the icy water. At St. Regis I swung due east, heading for Paradise. I was hungry and tired, and I stopped at the gas station in town and stocked up on coffee and cigarettes before driving out to my parents' place. It was late when I started down the back road toward the trailer.

There's a silence to winter here that is like nothing else. Animals that haven't headed south bed down in caves, tuck their heads under warm wings, nestle beneath thick snow. The few that don't sleep wander quiet as monks in a frozen prayer garden. When you come upon them, an owl in the black branches of an apple tree, a deer's face outside the glass of your bedroom window, their very presence is unnerving – like statuary come to life, or your own face caught unexpectedly in a mirror.

Though it was deathly cold, I drove the rough road to my parents' place with my windows open. Amos wasn't the only person to have died that day. After the initial shock, the horror of his murder faded and the gray face of Tina Red Deer came back to me, nagging and insistent. There is something about death, about the vacant body, hollow as an empty house, that begs for ownership, calls to be claimed. Now that Tina was gone I needed to know more than ever what was common between us. If it was true, if she was my father's daughter, he needed to be told.

I crept along as slowly and quietly as I could, aware of the clamor of my engine, the explosions of snow shaken from the boughs of pine trees. Just before the trailer came into view I crested a small hill and cut the engine and lights. The truck rolled forward, coasting the last few yards along the moon-silvered road. I passed my parents' driveway, pulling up alongside the split-rail fence that marked the edge of their property.

A wide field stretched beyond the fence, the snow on it deep, unblemished by footprints. Its surface had been sculpted by the wind into rolling dunes, like a sea caught in mid-undulation. The moon was newly risen, almost full, brighter even than the sun at this time of year. The sky was perfectly clear, littered with stars. At the far end of the field my parents' squat little trailer glowed like a camp lantern.

I took my binoculars from the glove compartment and watched my parents as I had watched them before. I wanted to go inside. That had been my intention in coming. But somehow I couldn't face my mother again. She served dinner, something thick that she ladled into deep bowls. She fed my father, her hand working in a strange rhythm. Bowl to spoon to mouth. She wiped his chin, set the napkin down. Her hair was pinned up tight around her head and she wore some kind of shapeless housedress with a repeating pattern of tropical flowers. I lit a cigarette and sipped at my cold coffee. I wanted her to leave. I wanted to see my father without her there. There must be somewhere she has to go, I told myself. Some prayer meeting. A quilting circle. A dress rehearsal for tomorrow's Christmas Eve pageant.

I watched her get up from the table and put the dishes in the sink. She turned the television on, propped my father on the couch, and disappeared from my view. I had no intention of going in now, but still I couldn't leave. I had Bennett's fancy parka on, the one I'd taken from the Big Sky Adventures office, but I was starting to shiver from the cold. I cranked the engine, turned the heater on. The ignition sounded loud as a gunshot.

After about fifteen minutes my mother's head came into view. She crossed into the kitchen area and reached for something high in a cupboard. Her hair was down, as I had not seen it for many years. It was thicker than ever, still red as a lit ember. She had changed into a green robe, silk or satin. It flowed around her wrists, dipped down in a deep V across her white chest. She pulled a bottle from the cupboard and poured herself a drink. Then she bent her head, cupped her hands in front of her face, and lit a cigarette.

I suppose I should have been surprised to see her like this, the person inside her like the raw and tender meat of an oyster. But I had always known who she was, how little she had changed. Watching her was as it had always been: magnetic terror, the dirty thrill of the voyeur. She moved across the trailer, skating from lit window to lit window, the green robe curving against her body like the Flathead flowing around a rock. She was beautiful as ever, exquisite and dangerous. I couldn't take my eyes off her.

It took almost two hours for her to drink herself into blackness. All that time my father sat in the living room, his head lolling from side to side, the blue light of the television flickering across his face. For a while my mother danced with herself. Then she sat at the table in the kitchen and cried. Eventually she put her head down. I lit a cigarette and watched her for a good five minutes. When she didn't move I got out of the truck and headed into the field.

The moon was still low enough to throw ghoulish shadows. The outlines of ponderosa pines stretched across the silver ground like long thin knives with jagged barbs. Halfway across the field I stopped to look back at my own shadow spread out on the ocean of snow. I raised my arms and watched my silhouette expand like a great, willowy bird.

Climbing the steps quietly, I opened the door and let myself inside. It was warm in the trailer, stuffy with cigarette smoke. A plate of cookies sat on the coffee table. Not trees this time but jolly Santa faces, the beards sparkling with red sugar. The lights on the plastic Christmas tree blinked on and off and on again. My mother shifted slightly, made a tiny moaning noise. Her robe had fallen open and her right breast spilled onto the table. How often did she do this? My father looked up at me, recognition flickering somewhere deep, deep in his eyes. His hands were set carefully in his lap. The cushions around him were dark with a wet stain. The smell of urine mingled with pine candles and cinnamon potpourri.

I went to the closet and found him a clean pair of pants, underwear. When I came out he was groping for the cookies, his hands fumbling uselessly. I hooked my arms under his shoulders, pulled him up from the piss-soaked couch, and undid his belt.

'Daddy,' I said, 'the Red Deer woman. Do you remember her?'

His breath on my face smelled childlike, of rancid milk, half-chewed food. He tilted his head back and stared at me.

'Red Deer,' I said again, loudly this time. 'The little girl. What was her name?' I grappled with his weight, slid his pants down, his damp underwear. The hair around his penis was gray and wispy, like cotton candy, sugar floss.

He gripped my shoulder and mumbled, his voice loud and agitated. I helped him out of his pants and into the clean ones. He took a step back from me while I buckled his belt, then stood there like a child dressed for church.

'Tina Red Deer?' I asked, handing him a Santa cookie.

He muttered again, put the cookie down, and limped into the bedroom, shaking his head.

In the drab little wood-paneled bedroom, my mother's housedress lay neatly on her side of bed. Her empty slippers waited patiently on a throw rug that read AWAKEN TO JESUS. My father's side of the bed was piled high with therapeutic pillows, chunks of foam rubber: the bed of an eighty-year-old man. My father was sixty-one.

I stood in the doorway and watched him. He opened his mouth and contorted his tongue, as if trying to form a word. He crossed the room and stood before a chest of drawers, made a spastic gesture that seemed to indicate he wanted me to follow. The top of the bureau was jammed with picture frames and small bottles, scraps of paper. It was a bizarre reliquary. A tiny baby tooth, the first one I lost, in a pill bottle. A lock of fine blond hair. My gap-toothed second-grade picture. A photo of my eighth-grade graduation. A poem about pumpkins I had written the Halloween I was ten.

And in the center of it all a picture of the three of us that had always been my mother's favorite. A friend of my parents had taken it at the fair the summer before the accident. It was a hot day and we were beautifully flushed, our faces healthy and tan. My mother had her arm around my father's waist, and you could see the shadow of her muscle working to hold him. Her hair was perfectly coiffed, held back by a loose ribbon. My father had his hands under my arms, as if about to lift me off the ground.

And he was. As soon as the shutter snapped he hoisted me up onto his shoulders so I could see the dizzying midway from above. It was a perfect picture, not static as most photographs are. Maybe that's why my mother liked it so much. There was the promise of motion in each of our poses. Even the background whizzed by. The lights of the tilt-a-whirl spinning out of focus, a little boy caught waving, a dart in midair on the way to its target.

With great effort my father grabbed the frame and lifted it off the dresser. I put my hand out to take it but he held it to his chest. He moved his mouth again, bent in close to my ear.

'Red . . . Deer,' he stammered, ripping the back off the picture frame. He held the backless frame out to me, worked his mouth again.

Behind the photograph of us was a second picture, smaller. I picked it up and studied the two dark faces on the slick paper, a woman and a child. The little girl's hair was plaited into two long braids. The woman's hair was long and black, stylishly curled. It made me think of the heroines of my childhood: Farrah Fawcett, Wonder Woman. The picture was taken outside, and behind them was the brown and gold expanse of the Great Plains. The woman was looking straight ahead, but the girl's eyes were tilted slightly upward, at the photographer.

Somehow the picture had survived all these years. I was certain that if my mother had known about it she would have destroyed it. But it had sat there, like a shadow behind the three of us, a last laugh at my mother's expense. My father's other family.

'She's gone,' I said, taking his hand in mine. Spittle glistened in the corners of his mouth. He fixed his eyes on mine. 'The girl . . . she's dead, Daddy.'

He flexed his hand, his nails digging into my palm. For a moment it seemed like his mind was fixed on the concept, that he understood what had happened. Then, suddenly, his train of thought evidently broken, he wandered into the living room.

I took the picture from the frame and stuffed it into the pocket of the parka. When I came out of the bedroom, my parents were both at the kitchen table. My mother was still in a state of semiconsciousness and my father pawed at her exposed breast. She opened one eye like a dangerous animal that had been drugged, looking up at me as I passed. I opened the door and stepped out into the cold night, leaving them as they were. Outside, the snow on the field had formed a fine skin of ice. I stuck to my old tracks going back to the truck.

Driving west through the mountains, all I could think about was running. I kept replaying Ivan and Amos as I had last seen them, kept picturing Josie, her body a vessel for danger. There was no real home for me in Missoula, no reason to stay. I ran through my options, old connections I could still call on for work, debts I was owed. I could even start over clean, I told myself, get a waitressing gig, go back to school.

At Superior, barely able to keep my eyes open, I wheeled off the highway and checked into a grungy little single-story motel. My room felt oddly comfortable: the bland furnishings in shades of rust and taupe, the proximity to the interstate, the neat little bottles of shampoo and conditioner, the bleached-out towels. Safer than Kristof's foreignness. Safer than the domesticity of Mrs. Carter's little house. It was the best kind of motel, lacking any local features that might pinpoint its location, completely void of character, with curtains thick enough to keep out most of the daylight. An oil painting over the bed showed a blue stream, trees in autumn, a stone bridge.

I dead-bolted the door, took my clothes off, and stepped into the shower, letting the hot water run until the bathroom was white with steam. I could head out in the morning, I told myself, after a good night's sleep. It was so tempting, the prospect of slipping away. I closed my eyes and felt the water on my back, the spray against my shoulder blades, against the knobs of muscles, against my spine. I used the miniature shampoo, the lilliputian soap.

After I'd dried myself I stepped back into the room, lit a cigarette, and lay on the bed. There was a mirror on the closet door and I could see my legs in it, my hips, the dark V of my pubis. I propped myself up on one elbow, watching the bowl of my stomach slacken where my pelvic bone pushed upward.

A semi roared by on the street outside, its engine grinding into low gear and then laboring up the on-ramp to the interstate. I put my cigarette out and slid my hands between my legs, imagining the gray ribbon of the highway, the blessed monotony of much of the American landscape, the eroticism of anonymity.

Through the wall I heard my neighbors turn their TV on, flip aimlessly through the channels, and turn it off. There must have been a moment of buoyancy, I thought, watching myself in the mirror, the shadows in my legs where the muscles contorted. A refusal of gravity in her last leap, then her body swinging, like a pendulum ticking off the seconds.

*You'll leave Missoula in the morning,* I reassured myself, but even as I said it I knew I would not go. When I closed my eyes I saw Kristof's face in Josie's photograph, his lips open and vulnerable, his cheeks exposed to the cold. And I saw Amos, his gangly limbs swinging through the crowd at Charlie's, his hands shaking over an unrolled cigarette, his mouth twisting into an uneven smile as he fingered the points of his Mohawk.

# Fifteen

It was late the next morning before the highway disgorged me back into Missoula. Coming in from the west, the thalassic history of the valley was clear. Houses washed up the southern hills like waves breaking on the shore of the prehistoric lake the valley had once been. Developments, like rivers or shimmering inlets, rushed up creek beds, spreading west into Idaho and north to the Flathead.

Amos's death was no coincidence. I wanted to find out why he'd been killed. I was hoping I might get lucky and make it to his place before his corpse was discovered and his trailer was crawling with cops. But the doughnut eaters were one step ahead of me. A crowd of them had gathered in the grungy little trailer park behind the Super Six. A half-dozen cop cars were massed in the motel's parking lot. From what I could see it was a typical police affair, lots of coffee drinking and aimless milling around. Figuring I'd try again later, I laid my foot on the accelerator and sped past the hospital toward the university.

It was winter break at the University of Montana, and the campus was nearly abandoned. Looping around behind the school, I pulled up in front of the main library. I slid Bennett's briefcase out from under my front seat, hooked my right arm around the gray metal, and climbed out into the cold. A sign on the front door said the library was closed but directed ambitious students to the law school. I made the long trek across the snowy campus, keeping my fingers crossed that they would have what I wanted.

The law school library was almost completely deserted. A few zombielike students wandered through the stacks. One girl in a study carrel lay with her head down, snoring loudly.

I asked a kid behind the front desk for back issues of the *Missoulian*.

He put down a dog-eared copy of *Forbes* magazine. 'How old?'

'Fifty-eight,' I told him.

'Microfilm,' he said, handing me a yellow slip of paper. 'Fill out this request form and I'll get it for you.'

I filled the form out, thought about the dates for a second, what Gloria had said about the plane crash. *March-September,* I wrote, and handed the paper to the kid.

'I'm only allowed to give you one month at a time,' he said, reading my request.

I looked around the empty library. 'You got a lot of people asking for forty-year-old *Missoulian* articles today?'

The kid shook his head, got up from his chair. 'It'll be a few minutes,' he grumbled.

Taking a seat at one of the microfilm readers, I

opened the briefcase and flipped aimlessly through Bennett's maps. The case was in bad shape, the lock twisted and mangled where Ivan had forced it open with a bullet. The fleur-de-lis lining on the inside was sagging in places, its edges shearing away from the metal lip that ringed the interior of the case. I took all the maps out, set them on the table, and ran my hand across the lining. The inside of the bottom of the briefcase was boxy, the corners squared. The top was rounded, the sides and corners sloping smoothly into each other. I peeled the fleur-de-lis lining away at the edges, revealing hard plastic backing on both halves of the case.

'Here you go.'

I looked up, momentarily startled, and saw the kid from the front desk. He held a stack of microfilm reels.

'Happy reading,' he said, setting the film on the table next to the reader. As he left, I laid the open case on the table next to the maps.

I hadn't been in a library since high school, and it took me a while to figure out how to work the microfilm machine. I fiddled with the knobs, scanning through March. Nothing. The third week of April, I found the first mention of the crash. AIR FORCE FLIER DISAPPEARS OVER BITTERROOTS, the headline read. It was front page news.

According to the article, Bennett had been on a solo flight in a T-33 training jet when he went down. He was a reserve officer, first lieutenant. There obviously hadn't been much information available at the time the article was written. The paper mentioned a spring blizzard and the possibility that the weather had had something to do with the crash. According to the *Missoulian,* the same snowstorm had hindered the search for the downed airman. I scribbled the name of the airplane he'd been in on a piece of scrap paper, made a photocopy of the article, and scrolled on through the microfilm.

A second article written a few days later detailed the Air Force's failure to find Bennett or his plane. Even with the weather clearing, the search was called off and Bennett was declared officially dead. 'We've done all we can,' an official was quoted as saying. I thought about what Jan Jorgenson had said at the dealership, how the pilots at Johnson-Belle hadn't seen any planes in the air. It had seemed strange to them that the Air Force would end the search so quickly, and it still did.

I scrolled on through the microfilm, skipping ahead to late June, looking for news of Bennett's miraculous return. 'DEAD' PILOT WALKS OUT OF BLODGETT CANYON, the *Missoulian* proclaimed. Just as Gloria said, Bennett was a hero. He insisted he'd been brought down by the storm but had managed to land the plane at a backcountry airstrip. His account of his time on the ground was muddled, foggy. He was half starved, he explained, living off a meager supply of canned food he found in a fire lookout, melting snow for water, yet he expressed no anger at having been left for dead.

'I knew I'd get out of it somehow,' he told a reporter. His smile in the accompanying photograph was spry and toothy.

One of the other officers from his reserve unit, a

George Dupres, was quoted as well. 'We all knew he was a survivor,' Dupres said.

It was peculiar: the aborted search and the way the papers glossed over it. It was almost as if the Air Force didn't want to find Bennett or the plane. Or maybe it wasn't the plane, but what was in the plane, the same thing Bennett had been looking for before he died, the same thing Ivan wanted, and Josie.

Something is very wrong, I told myself. I wondered if Tina had had the same thought at the instant the noose tightened around her neck. Something is very wrong. And Bennett, slipping down through the clouds toward the moment of impact, had he also spoken those words to himself?

I jotted Dupres's name down, made another photocopy, and flipped the microfilm machine off. Sliding my arms into my coat, I bent and piled the maps back inside the case. The top went down but stopped about an inch short of closing. I put my palm on the metal exterior and pressed, but it wouldn't shut. I flipped the case open again and ran my hand along the metal lip where the top and bottom fit together. The plastic backing on the inside of the top of the case had come loose and was slightly askew. I gave it a tug and it came free in my hands. Beneath the plastic was glue-streaked Styrofoam and, sealed in a Ziploc sandwich bag, the rectangular shape of a quad map.

Stopping short, I took a deep breath and looked around the library. The kid at the desk had gone back to his magazine. The girl was still sleeping in her carrel. Another girl, her back to me, flipped through a law journal. I lifted the plastic bag from the inside of the case, opened the zipper, and pulled the map out. It was the same area as the others, somewhere up the Bitterroots. In the lower right-hand corner, where an *N* and an arrow marked the direction of north, someone had taken a ballpoint pen and drawn a second arrow, this one almost perpendicular to the first.

I unfolded the map and laid it on the table next to the microfilm reader. There was a certain poetry to the folds of land and water on the map, to the web of names: Goat Heaven Peak, Wounded Doe Ridge, Barren Creek. And there was a poetry to the map itself, the metaphor of it, the translation of geography into flat symbols. Here the broken blue line of intermittent water. There the black square of a fire lookout.

A stain of pink oozed across the paper like a slow leak. The top edge covered Indian Meadows and the swell of Freezeout Mountain. Then the basin between Sponge Creek and Fish Lake Creek. At the bottom of the highlighted area sat Fish Lake, the blue of it turned purple with the pink ink. And next to the long thin lake, a cross of black.

If you believe that difference in language is one of the things that divides us, you also have to believe that the universal dialect of symbols somehow unites us. Ever since the first man put his muddy stick on the dark wall of a cave, the pointed roof of a tepee has meant shelter, the arching body of a fish has meant food. Yet here was one symbol that the early cartographer in his skins and furs would not have understood. He might have looked at the off-center cross and thought of a bird, or of an arrow sitting against the tight string of a bow. He might have imagined flight of some kind, the flint of an arrowhead whistling to its target, a V of geese lifting off a lake.

But having been born in the age of jet propulsion, in the era of moon walks and space shuttles, I knew at first glance what the tiny figure meant. It sat right on the edge of a lake, at a place where several faint trails intersected. There was so little to notice in the square of land that my eye picked it out immediately. It was the printed shape of an airplane, the mapmaker's indication of a landing strip.

I glanced back at the bottom of the quad, at the hand-penned arrow, and then folded the map and put it back in its bag.

I left the microfilm with the kid on the way out of the library, stepped into the foyer, slid a quarter into the pay phone, and dialed Ken Hoppie's pawnshop.

'Hey, Hop,' I said when he answered, 'what do you know about early jets?' Hop's an expert on all things having to do with the military, and I figured if anyone would know he would.

'Which one?'

'An Air Force trainer. From the fifties,' I explained, looking at the note I'd made. 'Called a T-Thirty-three.'

'What do you want to know?' Hop asked.

'How much is something like that worth?'

'Now?'

'Yeah.'

'Mint condition, to a collector, I'd say about twenty grand, why?'

'Just curious. What kind of cargo could a plane like that handle?'

'None.'

'Like none-at-all none?'

'Yeah. Zero cargo,' he repeated. 'It's a training jet, modeled on a fighter. I mean, I suppose anything's possible, but you'd have to strip that baby down if you wanted to carry something. It'd hardly be a T-Thirty-three anymore.'

'But it's possible?'

'Sure.'

'Thanks,' I told him, not sure if he'd helped or not.

I hung up the phone with Hop and dialed Nick Popov's Hot Springs place. Vera answered on the second ring.

'Ivan's treasure hunt,' I said. 'How much money are we talking about?'

Vera drew her breath in, made a fast recovery. 'You must never to phone here,' she hissed.

'Good. Let's make a deal. You tell me and I won't bother you again. How much? Thousands? Millions?'

'Millions,' she told me.

I heard a click, and the line went dead.

*Paranoia will destroy ya*. It's the pot smoker's mantra. When I was in high school, my friend Stacy and I used to ditch school and go down to the river bottom and get loaded. Stacy's parents were rich ex-hippies who had started a natural food business and made enough to retire on at forty. By the time Stacy was thirteen she had found their stash box and was helping herself to their best sticky bud. Back then I had a preference for liquor. While Stacy fumbled through her parents' underwear drawer, I would go down to the Food Farm and have Billy Craighead, the retarded man who sold newspapers out front, go inside and buy me a six-pack.

I don't know why we found it necessary to go down to the river. It's not like our parents would have cared much. My mother was always at the church. I could have tattooed my entire face with the devil and she wouldn't have noticed. And Stacy's mother and father spent their days blissed out in the Jacuzzi, grooving to old Motown records, reliving their free-love years.

The river bottom was a spooky place. There was dense brush and cottonwood thickets, places for people to hide. Except during the coldest months of the winter, there were always bums camped in the trees. Sometimes we would work ourselves into a frenzy of anxiety, imagining we had been discovered. That's when Stacy would start up with her singsong rhyme.

*Paranoia will destroy ya.* I said the words out loud as I crossed the river and headed along Broadway toward Amos's place. Josie's face kept repeating itself in my mind, Amos's naked body in the snow. Whatever he had done, he hadn't deserved to die like he did. There was no sign of police presence in the grubby trailer park, so I pulled around back of the Super Six and parked next to an overflowing Dumpster.

There was a futuristic quality to the makeshift neighborhood that had sprung up between the motel and the river. These trailers made my parents' place truly look like paradise. But even the crudest dwellings, crank-up truck toppers with no sign of toilet facilities, had cable hookups or even mini-satellite systems. Televisions glimmered beyond frost-pale windows.

Several sad attempts at Christmas decorating had been made. A four-foot candy cane glowed red and white next to the front steps of one of the larger trailers. A plastic Christmas tree with a clown face shook its limbs as I passed by and broke into a chorus of 'Jingle Bells.' The poverty and decay mixed with modern technology and tackiness re-minded me of a bad apocalypse movie. America after World War Three. Mel Gibson scouring what used to be the fallow fields of the Midwest for a last gallon of gasoline, a pack of cigarettes.

It had turned out to be a bright day, but the sun provided only meager warmth. Under the parka, I was wearing a pair of wool-lined Carhartt pants, silk long underwear, two sweaters, and my pac boots. With all the layers I was like an abdomen-heavy beetle. One push and I would have been on my back, unable to help myself up. The cold bit at the few raw places on my body where skin was exposed.

I made my way to Amos's silver Airstream, the rubber soles of my Sorels squealing against the dry packed snow. Yellow crime-scene tape crisscrossed the yard like silk from a larger-than-life atomic spider. A half-dozen feral-looking boys were playing on the rusted carcass of an old farm truck in the weeds next to Amos's place. Their coats were thin and ragged, unzipped to reveal T-shirts. Only one was wearing gloves, oversized hand-me-downs that made his fists look like giant lobster claws.

The boys were playing a loud game of shoot-'em-up and didn't take much notice as I passed by. It wasn't till I'd pushed open the chain-link gate on Amos's fence and ducked under the yellow tape and into his yard that I felt the dull thud of a shattered snowball on the back of my right shoulder.

'He's dead,' a voice said behind me.

Turning, I faced my attacker, a big kid, maybe ten or eleven, burly and blotchy-faced.

'Oh, yeah?'

The kid sniffled and swiped at his nose with the back of his hand. 'You a friend?' he asked suspiciously.

I nodded. 'I left something here. Just came by to pick it up.'

'You got a key?' he asked.

I wasn't sure how to answer. I stared at the kid for a minute, then turned my back to him and started for the door of the trailer.

'Ten bucks!' he yelled. I could hear his feet crunching on the snow, then he was next to me.

'Ten bucks for what?' I asked.

'To let you in.' He shrugged, pulled a key from his coat pocket, and held it between his thumb and forefinger.

'Where'd you get that?'

'None of your damn business. You want in or what?'

I fished in my pocket and pulled out a wadded-up five-dollar bill. 'It's all I've got,' I told him.

'You're lying,' the kid snapped.

He was right, but I made a move like I was about to put the fiver away. 'Take it or leave it,' I said nonchalantly.

The kid's fingers darted out and grabbed the bill. He glared at me. 'Fucking cheapskate.'

I followed his small back up the rotting stairs on the side of the trailer. He unlocked the door and pushed it open, motioning for me to enter. The shades were drawn and it was dark inside. Several furry shapes darted back and forth in the shadows. The air coming out of the trailer reeked of excrement and animal nests.

Taking a step backward, I cupped my hand over my nose.

'Ferrets,' the kid explained. 'Amos gave me the key so I could take care of them when he wasn't around. Most of them got out this morning when the cops were here. They're probably frozen now. They won't hurt you.'

He looked at me skeptically, his eyes taking in the bruise on my face, the false bulk of my clothing.

'You going in or what?'

Though outsiders are constantly astonished by the string of antigovernment groups that Montana produces, the preponderance of crazies has never surprised me. When I was growing up, Montana was a state of have-nots, a place where almost everyone was scraping to get by. Except for a few wealthy Californians and New Yorkers who have moved in, nothing much has changed.

In other places it's easy to pick your enemy by skin color. There is a rainbow of other races on which to pin blame. In the West, where almost every face is white, the options are fewer. But people here are resourceful and have learned to focus their hatred. They dislike out-of-staters and tax collectors. And though they'd never admit it, they dislike the Indians. I could see it on the kid's face as he watched me, this swelling scar of distrust and hostility. I could see the shabby beginnings of what Amos had become, the infant rage.

'What's your name?' I asked, fumbling for some kind of connection, wishing I could say the right thing to ignite the tiniest fire of mutual understanding.

The kid turned his head and spit. The door to a neighboring trailer popped open and an ashy-faced woman leaned her head out and bawled. The boys on the truck scattered and the kid leapt off the stairs and disappeared.

Stepping into the Airstream, I ran my fingers along the inside wall until I found the nub of the light switch. The electricity blazed on and the ferrets scampered from the glare of the overhead bulb. The trailer was tiny and cramped, just one room with a kitchenette and small bathroom in the back. The walls were plastered with a strange mix of art: soft-core pictures of tanned women in bikinis; a New Age portrait of Jesus with golden rays streaming from his head; bowling posters signed by soft-bellied world champions I've never heard of. Most of the space was taken up by video equipment: a brand-new television, two VCRs, a couple of videocameras. The entire far wall was stacked high with videotapes. A purple vinyl bag sat on the floor, a blue marbled bowling ball peeking out from its open mouth.

One of the cameras was mounted on a tripod, its lens pointing toward the trailer's small side window. I stepped forward, bent my head, and carefully put my eye to the viewfinder. A window appeared, floral curtains pulled shut, cream-colored cinder block: the back side of the Super Six Motel. Somehow I wasn't surprised by Amos's voyeurism. I scanned the rooms on the first floor, stopping at the first open curtains I came across. The overhead light was on in the room and I could clearly make out a figure lying on the bed, two stockinged feet, hands crossed over chest. The television squirmed with tiny figures.

Taking my eye from the viewfinder, I popped the small hatch that would have held the camera's cassette. It was empty. I stood back from the camera and stared out the window at the back of the motel. If Amos had been watching, I told myself, he could have seen everything that happened in Bennett's room that day. Shrouded as they are by brush and cottonwood, you wouldn't necessarily notice the trailers from the motel, wouldn't think there might be someone watching. Turning from the window, I stepped across the trailer and edged closer to the shelves of video tapes.

Most of the cassettes were marked MCAT, the public-access station that aired *Anarchy with Amos*. Above the MCAT videos was a large collection of pornos. From what I could see, Amos's taste was rather eclectic. *Hot and Horny Asians* sat next to a rubber and PVC fetish flick titled *Bared and Bound*. To the left of the adult section were two neatly alphabetized shelves of more mainstream fare. It was mostly sci-fi stuff: two copies of *Dune*; the director's cut of *Blade Runner*; some old *Star Trek* TV shows; a recent horror movie I happened to see at the drive-in last summer. Fairly typical for a guy like Amos. But there, filed under *B*, a title caught my eye.

Funny, I thought, maybe anarchists are sentimental at heart. Maybe it's some strange sense of nostalgia and romanticism that drives them. But I didn't think so. I slipped off my mittens, pulled the oblong box out and turned the cover over. *The Bridges of Madison County*, it read, dark letters on a pale background. Meryl Streep looked up into the lean face of Clint Eastwood, her eyes shimmering with checked tears.

I tried to picture Amos with his feet propped up on the grease-stained ottoman, a bottle of Night Train in one hand and a box of Kleenex in the other. I tried to see him in his ratty La-Z-Boy, his heart tuned to the tale of unfulfilled love, his eyes pink-rimmed and puffy, his fingers stroking the silky back of one of his ferrets. Somehow the scene just didn't wash.

I slipped the black tape from the *Bridges of Madison County* box. It was noticeably lighter in my hand than a regular videotape. The guts of the cassette had been ripped out, leaving a hollow shell. I lifted the flap where the tape would have been and peered inside. Far in the back was a small key. A slip of paper hung from a hole in the metal head. I dumped the key into my palm. The number 46 was stamped into it, as if it opened something in a public place – say, a locker at a bus station or gym. On the tiny scrap of paper someone had written one word. LIBERTY, it said, the letters penned in red ink.

A car door slammed outside. Slipping the key in my pocket, I turned and started for the door. One of the ferrets was pacing the entryway, its belly gliding along the ground. The animal stopped and faced me, curled its tiny lips, and bared its sharp little teeth. I grabbed a broom, ready to slap it out of my way, but before I was halfway through my swing I heard the plaintive squeak of shoes on the walk.

My first thought was that it was Chief Riley, or the kid come back to hustle me for some more money. I caught a glimpse of the dark top of an adult-height head bobbing across the side window of the trailer. For a split second I was frozen in place; then my mind raced over my options and I headed for Amos's cramped bathroom.

The ferrets had been particularly active in the bathroom. Tufts of brown fur lined the shower stall. The linoleum was peeled away, gnawed at the edges. I reached into my pocket, eased the Sig out, and wedged myself into the space between the open door and the wall. I heard the visitor pound up the steps to the trailer, then the panicked scuffling of the ferrets as the person stepped inside.

Even before she spoke I knew it was a woman. She had doused herself in cheap perfume, and its stench wafted to me over the rancid smell of the trailer. Her movements were careful, quiet. The floor creaked as she stepped across the main room. I could hear her rummaging through drawers and cupboards, haphazardly searching.

Leaning my back against the wall, I peered through the narrow slit where the door swung back from its hinges. I could see a strip of Amos's sink, crusted dishes piled high. My clothes, which were barely comfortable outside, were stifling. Sweat rolled down my chest, sliding against the silk of the long johns. One of the ferrets flitted across the doorway and I felt a sinking in my pelvis, a flash of fear that made me think I might wet myself. I was picturing Amos as I had last seen him, and I wondered if I should jump out with the Sig blazing.

She paced back and forth, crossing my line of view briefly, long enough for me to confirm what I suspected. It was Josie. She was so close I could smell her sweat underneath the sharp tang of her perfume. It was a distinctly female odor, musky like the dirty pelts of the ferrets, acrid and salty.

Her nails brushed across the flimsy pressboard of the bathroom door, as if she knew I was there. I inhaled slowly, feeling the air catch in my lungs, then shifted the barrel of the Sig till it was just in front of my chest. I bit down on my lower lip, waiting for her to make the first move. She sniffed at the air, took a step back.

'Hey! Hey, you!' It was the kid's voice, shrill and adolescent. It startled me and I twitched, my boots scuffling against the door. I heard her move away.

'Fuck off,' Josie said.

'You fuck off, lady. No pay, no entry.' His voice was slightly distant, dulled.

Stepping to the small window of the bathroom, I pressed my cheek to the glass. I could see the kid on the front porch, his leather basketball shoes kicking at the iced snow. He took a step forward, placing one foot over the threshold, then stopped.

'C'mon, lady. Time to go.'

I shimmied to the door of the bathroom and pivoted around, pressing my forearm against the jamb, aiming for the base of Josie's skull. Her back was to me, and beyond her I could see the front of the kid's shin, his one shoe pressed into the carpet. 'Just go,' I whispered, my finger trembling over the Sig's trigger.

She drummed her fingers against her thigh, rubbed at the side of her hip, her hands contemplating action. Then she turned her head, glanced quickly in my direction, and moved for the door. Skirting back to the window, I watched the kid saunter toward Amos's makeshift fence and put his hand proprietarily on the cold metal of the gate. Josie followed, her arm brushing his coat open as she passed. His T-shirt was one size too small, the cotton plastered across the soft flesh of his stomach. She stopped in front of him and peered down, searching his face.

Through the haze of filth that coated the bathroom window I could just barely see the kid's eyes, the lids opened wide to reveal bright whites. He pursed his lips and spit, spraying Josie's face. I was certain she was going to slap him, but she didn't. Instead she moved off, slid in behind the wheel of her blue Malibu, and gunned away.

The kid was still there at the gate when I left, his eyes on the tracks her car had made. I reached into my pocket, pulled out two twenty-dollar bills, and handed them to him. It was all I had.

# Sixteen

My first thought when I pulled the key from the empty cassette in Amos's trailer was that the lock it opened was somewhere public: a bus station, maybe, or an airport, or a gym. Why else the two digits stamped into the key's metal head? I envisioned rows of numbered lockers, the forty-sixth opening itself to me.

The Greyhound station was just a few blocks from Amos's, and it was my first stop after I left the trailer. I found a locker number 46, but the key wasn't even close to being a fit.

I left the bus station and sped out to the airport, my mind skipping from the empty landscape to a different kind of emptiness, to the peculiar form of absence that liquor can bring. Wind knifed across the side of the Ford and I gripped the wheel, struggling to stay on the road. I focused on the black line of the asphalt and on a few forgotten moments at the Super Six Motel.

The television was on, I told myself, an afternoon soap opera providing a soft campfire glow in the dark room. Whatever the on-screen characters were up to – sex, revenge, business schemes – probably meant little to the trio of drinkers. Their only concern was the dwindling supply of malt liquor and the long walk to the convenience store across the street. Colt 45. Schlitz. Tiger 500. I ran through the beverage options in my mind, wanting to fit the details into place.

Let's say they were down to their last forty-ouncer. Tina was starting to get cranky, and Bennett felt unsure of his ability to hold the buzz. Someone was elected to go fetch more supplies. Maybe the three pooled their money; maybe Elton was still feeling lucky from a surprise win at the keno machine and decided to spring for the next round.

This is where Tina and Elton blacked out. What happened in the next half hour was lost to the dark haze of amnesia. They stumbled out the door and across the street. Maybe they even passed her on their way; maybe she watched them cross the parking lot before making her way to Room 109. She knocked, and when Bennett opened the door she was there on the breezeway, a woman, heavy and dark. Did he think it a lucky break, this gift of a female? Did he stand there a moment, pondering the possibilities?

This was when she hit him. I envisioned one short disabling punch to the gut and then the knife slicing through his chest like a zipper cleaving the front of a coat. I imagined it was surprisingly painless at first. Bennett teetered for a moment, his legs gone rubbery beneath him. He looked down and saw the dark rip of the stain on the checkered cloth of his shirt. The smell of her was in his nose, sweat sharpened by adrenaline, the astringent fetor of her perfume. Then her hand was on him and she pushed him back through the door and onto the bed. She cut him again and again.

The parking lot of Johnson-Belle Field was deserted. The morning flight from the east had come and gone hours earlier, and the late flight from the west wouldn't get in until almost midnight. I pulled the Ford into the loading zone and pushed through the revolving doors into the warmth of the plush new terminal.

When I was a child there had only been the runway cutting across washed-out cattle land and a rickety trailer that had served as ticket counter and baggage claim. The new building seemed outlandish, far too large for the two or three flights a day it had been built to accommodate. Stuffed bobcats surveyed the cavernous waiting room. A wolf in a glass case attacked a bull elk with a rack the size of a small car. The animals were frozen in battle, bodies contorted, teeth bared, glass eyes open wide. Canned Christmas carols echoed through the empty building. 'God Rest Ye Merry, Gentlemen.' Plastic trees bristled under tinsel and lights like angry porcupines. Two security guards played gin rummy on the X-ray machine.

I asked about lockers and one of them looked up, waved lazily. 'Just past the bar.'

This time there wasn't even a number 46 to check the key against. Discouraged, I headed back out through the empty terminal, braced myself for the wind, and made a mad dash for my truck. I settled into the cab, cranked the heat up, and lit a cigarette.

A private plane approached from the south, swung into a wide bank, and bounced onto the runway, kicking a flurry of powder up behind its tail. I watched it roll along and nose into a slot next to a couple dozen other small prop planes. The door swung open and the pilot hopped out. There's only one airport in Missoula, and I figured Clay Bennett's plane had to be among the aircraft parked on the tarmac. Shifting into drive, I eased the truck out from the curb and headed away from the main terminal.

What is it about possessions? Do they hint at truths about the people who own them? Do we leave behind some part of ourselves that's more substantial than the invisible skin of cells our hands shed? I remember casting a spell on a boy I longed for in eighth grade: a schoolgirl's black magic, something to make him like me back. For the spell to work I needed as many of his belongings as possible. Things he'd fingered again and again. Clothes he'd worn. I broke into his locker, stole some pencils, a comb, a wool ski hat with a bright tassel on top.

It was this same kind of desire that drove me out across the grounds of the airport toward the clutch of small planes – a belief in objects, in the detritus of a life. I wanted to see the plane Clay Bennett had flown, the seat where he'd sat. I wanted him to reveal himself to me, for the mystery of his death to unravel.

Just a few lights were on in the small-aircraft hangar. I parked by the front door and got out. It was god-awful cold, savage, and I pulled the hood of Bennett's parka tight over my head. I knocked hard, thinking I might ask the lone pilot to point Bennett's plane out to me. I supposed I could tell him I was looking to buy.

No one answered and I cupped my hands to the glass, peered inside. My breath collected on the door, solidified immediately into an opaque circle of frost. I knocked once more, waited. The wind was blowing hard now, gusting out of the canyon on the far side of the valley. A truck passed on the highway, and in the silence that followed I heard voices, snippets of windblown speech, from the back of the hangar.

Bracing myself, I looked out from under my hood and started around the building. The side-ways force of the wind slammed into my ankles. When I rounded the hangar and stepped out into the open, I recognized Harry Ford and his Sikorsky chopper immediately. I'd known Harry since grade school. He'd always had a reputation as the bad kid, and he'd done his best to uphold this distinction. Each year he was the first kid to get sent to the principal's office, and he often spent recess at his desk. He lived just up the street from us when I was a kid. His dad was a smokejumper and his mom worked as a cashier at the Safeway.

After school Harry went into the army. He flies for the Forest Service now, fighting fires during the summer. Every Christmas Eve, Harry hooks up a lighted version of Santa and his team of reindeer and flies them around town. I'm not one for Christmas kitsch, and normally I would be irritated by the cheeriness of it all, but besides being a hell of a pilot, Harry's one of the biggest stoners in Missoula. The thought that he's up there smoking some fat bowls with his girlfriend, Cherise, puts a happy spin on the whole thing.

The helicopter sat parked on the tarmac now, while Harry and another parka-clad figure scurried around the tail. Evidently the wind had dislodged Santa and his reindeer from the back of the chopper. The two men struggled with lights and rope while Santa smiled stoically, his hands still firm on his painted reins.

'Harry!' I yelled, cupping my hands to be heard over the wind.

Harry looked up and grinned, motioning me closer. 'Hook us in, will ya?' he bellowed, pointing to a hitch on the back of the Sikorsky.

I grabbed the metal cord that hung off Santa's sleigh and secured him to the helicopter. Harry wrestled a two-dimensional Rudolph to the ground and laid a rock on the animal's head to secure it. He waved his helper off, and the second man bolted for the warmth of the hangar.

'Jesus, Mary, and Joseph!' Harry yelled, taking my mittened hand in his own. 'Let's get inside!'

It was hot in the private-aviation building, luxuriously warm. The second man waved to Harry, collected his belongings, and was gone. Harry pulled a pipe from his breast pocket, lit the bud inside, and took a long toke.

'You getting ready for tonight?' I asked.

'Just came out to make sure everything was okay in the wind.' Harry offered me the pipe. I shook my head. 'Christmas Eve,' he said. 'Can't not fly on

Christmas Eve.' He took a second toke, exhaled. 'Fucking wind, man,' he whispered absently, offering me the pipe again.

I lit a cigarette and propped my thighs against a gray metal desk. We were in the office part of the building. 'Hey, Harry,' I said. 'You knew Clay Bennett.'

'Sure.' Harry whistled. 'Christ, he got slashed up something bad, huh?'

I nodded. 'Is his plane still out here?'

'Right there,' Harry said. He pointed to a wide glass window that looked out on the darkened hangar. ''Cept it's not his no more.'

I could just barely make out a slice of white wing, black numbers on the cabin. 'Guess you can't take it with you,' I remarked, assuming that was what Harry had meant.

Harry looked at me solemnly, evidently contemplating the prospect of death. He lit a match and took another toke. 'Clay sold it before he got himself killed. Couple weeks before.'

'He upgrade for work?' I asked, taking a few steps closer to the window. There was a toolbox beneath the plane's nose and a mechanic's rolling stepladder.

'Unh-unh.' He shook his head, paused. 'The plan was to retire. Life's a bitch that way sometimes.'

I looked out at the shadowed plane and let what Harry said sink in. I thought about the map in the Ziploc bag and about the pink shading, the airstrip, and the oval of Fish Lake. You don't look for something all your life, I told myself, and give up before you've found it.

Harry came over and stood next to me. 'You want to go up in the Sikorsky tonight? No good to be alone on Christmas Eve.'

I shook my head. 'You ever been to Fish Lake?' I asked.

'Up in the Selway?'

'Yeah.'

'Flown over it. Why?'

'Is there still an airstrip there?'

'Supposed to be. Why?'

I shrugged. 'You think you could take me up there sometime?'

Harry beamed. 'Whenever you want.'

It was the tail end of the afternoon when I left the airport. Maybe three o'clock and already the light was skewed, baleful. The blank side of Mount Sentinel was lit full on by the setting sun. The fire road that ran the width of the mountain stood out in harsh relief, a long black scar on the white hillside. Pine trees in the high drainages looked like they'd been candied with bright sugars, orange and pink. In the west, pungent and skunklike, a veil of smoke streamed out of the paper mill.

One of the inmates I worked with in the laundry in New Mexico was a tiny little woman named Teddy Bear. She was originally from Atlanta but had been sent up for shooting her pimp down in Las Cruces. She hadn't killed him – though, according to her, she had succeeded in shooting both his testicles off.

The week before I got out she asked me where I was planning to go. Home, I said, and I told her about Montana. She was folding a sheet, and I remember she brought it across her chest so that the fabric snapped open. 'Uh-huh,' she said, as if I had just told her they were serving us surf and turf for dinner that night.

She was right to be skeptical. There's no greater conjurer than the chasm of separation, the desire to return to the place of our expulsion. What we call *missing* has very little to do with ourselves and everything to do with the thing from which we are divided, the way it acts upon us. Sometimes it is better not to go back, better not to find yourself homesick in the place that should be your home.

As I drove back toward town that day, the Missoula valley seemed as foreign to me as a lunar landscape. But in the green Eden of my memory flakes fell and fell past my window, settled on the ice of Rattlesnake Creek. I heard the furnace start, the rush of warm air snaking up through the vents, through the clean rooms of our old stone house. My bedroom door opened and I could smell bacon and buckwheat, the piney tang of evergreens. I sat up in bed and my father moved toward me, his wool socks scratching on the wood floor. I was five, maybe six. Small enough that when he lifted me up and I fitted my head against the side of his neck, I could just barely get my legs around his waist.

It is dangerous to think about these things: the way it feels to be carried; the particular weight of a hand on your head; the exact combination of smells – aftershave, shampoo, pancakes. I pushed the thoughts back, kept my eyes glued to the road.

Except for a few straggling shoppers, the streets of downtown were quiet. As I cruised north past the courthouse and the neon lights of the bail bondsmen, I thought of Tina and of Elton Williams. Drunken Indian, I told myself. I could see him scrabbling at the metal of his cell door, dreaming of the first quart of Strawberry Boone's Farm he'd tasted, the sugar on his tongue, the liquor rocketing to his brain. I wanted him to wake up and remember the moments he had forgotten, the time in which someone other than Tina had killed Clay Bennett.

I pulled up at the red light on Higgins, closed my eyes, and thought about Christmas in New Mexico: the familiar tray of soggy stuffing, processed turkey flecked with gristle and bits of marrow, a ring of cranberry jelly on the side. And the waiting room: kids brought in to see their mothers, a plastic tree, prison gifts of soap and cigarettes.

A horn sounded behind me. I opened my eyes and rolled forward.

Rattlesnake Creek was frozen solid. The ice roiled over boulders and slammed into the pancake of the Clark Fork River, pushing against itself, heaving upward in thick slabs. I parked my truck on the little stone bridge next to Kristof's and got out. The Sig was heavy in my pocket. The barrel knocked against my thigh. I was happy to see a light in Kristof's living room window. It was early for him to be home, but I figured they'd knocked a few hours off his shift for the holidays. From down below I could just make out his poster of the Prague

Castle: dark stone streaked with a city's grime, sharp roofs, spires twisting into a bleak sky.

I climbed the front stairs, opened the door, and stepped into the common foyer. It was a strange building, slightly makeshift. One apartment up and one down. The stairwell to Kristof's was dark and steeply pitched. Heavy piano music sounded from above: long-drawn-out chords, then abrupt silence.

It was stupid of me to have come and I knew it, but I was tired. I wanted to rest my head in the wing of Kristof's collarbone, put my hands on the two berms of muscle in his back. I wanted to stand at the window and watch the snow shift, to be grateful for warmth and cover. I took the last step and paused on the landing, shaking snow from my boots. The music started up again, serious, exotic.

As I put my hand on the knob, the door to Kristof's apartment jerked open and a hand grabbed my mouth. A thick arm tightened around my neck and I tasted leather, smelled the sour stench of cigar smoke. I flailed my arms, grappled with the wool coat of my assailant. He lifted his forearm from my throat, grabbed the soft hair at the base of my neck, and jerked, wrenching my head up to the light.

Nick Popov stood at the far end of the room. He looked over at me, pursed his lips into a neat circle, and lifted the spit-darkened end of his cigar from his mouth. He wore a brown coat and a brown fedora. Even here in Montana he dressed in that strangely formal Eastern European way. I felt the muscles in my legs slacken with fear.

'Rachmaninoff,' he said. 'A Russian. The only

one here.' He gestured to Kristof's stacks of CDs and vinyl. 'They don't like us, you know, the Czechs. But even they can't resist Rachmaninoff.'

The music stopped and the needle picked itself up off the turntable and returned to its cradle. It was quiet in the apartment and I could hear the tobacco in Popov's cigar burning when he inhaled. He walked to the side window and looked down over the frozen creek.

'In the matter of my son,' he said, clearing his throat.

The man holding me released my head and slid his hand down across my side. He put his fingers in the pocket of my parka and eased the Sig out, pressed the barrel to the side of my head.

My stomach flipflopped, and I thought I might be sick. Jeff Riley and the doughnut eaters were one thing. At worst they could send me back where I came from, make my life miserable for a few more years. But Nick Popov was another matter altogether. Only Josie scared me more. If Nick thought I'd had something to do with Ivan's death, the chances of my walking out of that apartment alive were slim to none.

I gasped once. The man holding me loosened his grip and I fell forward onto all fours, the skin of my palms rasping against the wood floor. I kept my head down, watched Popov's wing tips cross the floor and stop right in front of me.

'I didn't have anything to do with that,' I wheezed.

Popov raised his shoe and I tightened the muscles in my abdomen, ready to absorb the blow. But he didn't kick me. Instead, he put his sole gently on my side and pushed me over, so that my back was on the floor. The man in the wool coat bent down, keeping my gun close to my head.

Nick Popov shrugged his shoulders, gesturing to the man with the gun. 'I don't believe you two have been formally introduced. Megan Gardner, meet Gregor. Gregor, Meg.'

Gregor curled his lips up in an imitation of a smile.

'I didn't kill him,' I said, starting to panic.

Popov shook his head. He rested his hands on his knees and bent down. 'I believe you.' He smiled. 'Would you like to know why? You're smart, Meg.' He tapped his finger against the side of his head, pantomiming the word. 'You've thought this through, I'm sure. And you've realized I will find out sooner or later. That's where the smarts come in. See, if you were stupid you might lie to me. But you're smart enough to know what I'd do. You following me?'

I blinked once, nodded slowly.

'Good,' Popov continued. 'I think you might have an idea who did it. Am I right?'

I nodded again.

Gregor pushed the cold metal of the Sig into the hollow just below my ear. I could feel the circle of the barrel, the space in the middle where a bullet might come from.

'What is it you say?' He thought for a moment, then smiled, pleased with himself. 'I'm all ears.'

'There's a woman,' I told him. 'If I had to guess, I'd say she's a professional.'

'Who's she working for?'

'I don't know.'

'Where can I find her?' Popov asked.

I shook my head. 'She found me at Charlie's,' I said. 'Wanted something that was in Clay Bennett's car. Thought I might have taken it.'

'What does she look like?' Nick snapped.

'Like trouble,' I said. 'She's big . . . got a red dragon tattooed on her chest, dark hair.'

Nick took a long drag off the cigar and tossed the soggy stub on the floor.

'I believe you,' he said, standing.

Gregor took the gun from beneath my ear and slid the grip into my palm. He flashed me his jackal smile again; then they both disappeared through the doorway and down the stairs.

# Seventeen

I didn't get up right away. After Popov and Gregor left I lay with my back on the hard wood of the floor and stared up at the raised pattern of whorls that fanned across the ceiling. I listened to the two sets of Russian feet descending the stairs, to the car door slamming outside. Somehow the cold here makes noises crisper than usual, clearer. As if sound were something molecular, something that expands and contracts with the temperature. Popov's engine started confidently, hummed down the street. Some students passed on the sidewalk. I heard a snippet of a dirty joke, laughter. A fence clanged shut. A dog barked.

I lay there until the very last of the daylight left the valley. Until the lights of the city reflected off the low underbelly of the cloud cover and the sky outside the window turned a dull industrial henna, like the dimpled base of a well-used copper pot. I got up slowly, my return to the living beginning to sink in. My fingers were tight on the Sig. The pattern of the grip was etched into my palm.

I found some vodka in the kitchen and took a long swig from the bottle. I fished in the pocket of my parka for the articles I'd copied earlier at the library. I read the stories again, reread them. Bennett had flown out of Fairchild Air Force Base that day, just over the mountains, near Spokane. He was a reserve officer, which meant he couldn't have been far from home. I lit a cigarette, picked up the phone, and dialed information for Spokane, Washington.

'Bennett,' I told the operator, when she asked for a name.

'First name?'

I thought about the question for a moment, my eyes skimming the articles. I'd been hoping to find a relative, but it was a ridiculous idea and I knew it.

'Ma'am?' the operator broke in. 'There are ninety-eight Bennetts listed in the Spokane area. Do you have a first name?'

'No, sorry . . . wait. Can you try Dupres? George Dupres.' It was the only other name mentioned in either of the articles, and I figured it was worth a shot.

'Spokane again?'

'Yes.'

A keyboard clicked in the background; then the line switched over and a mechanical voice chimed George Dupres's number. I scratched the digits in the lower margin of the article, disconnected from information, and dialed.

The phone rang four times on the other end before a tiny child's voice answered.

'Is George Dupres there?' I asked.

I heard the receiver bang against the floor, small feet running, and a far-off cry. 'Daddy!'

Shoes shuffled across carpet. Someone sighed into my ear. 'Hello?'

'Mr. Dupres?'

'Yes?'

I cleared my throat, wishing I'd planned out what I was going to say. 'You don't know me, sir. I just ran across your name in an old newspaper article.'

'Oh?' The voice was wary, distant.

I scrambled to think of an excuse for calling, lit on the lie I'd told Gloria O'Keefe. 'I work for an aviation club out here in Montana,' I explained. 'I'm writing a kind of memorial for one of our members, Clayton Bennett. I think you used to fly with him.'

'Fly, as in an airplane?' the man asked.

'Yes.'

'I think you've got the wrong George Dupres, miss.'

'Oh.' Disappointment snapped like a rubber band in my chest. 'I'm sorry to have bothered you.'

'No bother.' I heard his hand rustle against the mouthpiece, then, 'Dad? I think it's for you.'

'For me?' It was an older man's voice this time, muffled by distance.

'Yeah,' the son replied. 'Some woman. Wants to ask you something about flying.'

The phone was handed over and the older voice came on the line. 'Yes?'

I launched into my cover story again, explaining the purpose of my call.

'And what exactly do you want from me?' the older Dupres asked when I finished talking.

'Just anything you remember. About the crash in particular. Or old friends I might call.'

He paused for a moment, his breath rasping into the phone. 'He wasn't really tight with any of us – except our squad leader, of course: rich kid out of California. Big snob. It was him that went out looking after Clay went down. Him and only him. Flew out to Fish Lake in the storm all by himself. Said he checked that airstrip and didn't find nothing.'

'I understand none of you went out after the storm broke?'

'We wanted to,' Dupres continued. 'Like him or not, Bennett was one of us. But they called the search off, said there was nothing to be done. Where'd you say you're calling from?'

'Montana.'

'So you know how it is, then. The weather. I guess the feeling was he didn't stand a chance out there. We were sure happy to see him come out alive. Of course, he quit the reserves after that.'

'Your squad leader?' I asked. 'Do you remember his name?'

'Sure, I remember his name. He's back in California. San Jose, I think. Like I said, Harvey and Clay were best buddies.'

'Harvey?'

'Yeah, Harvey Eckers. Wouldn't you know it? Guy's a politician now. Seems perfect. Though that business with his uncle seems to be catching up with him. What was his name . . . ?' Dupres mused. 'Senator something. To tell you the truth, that's why we never really liked him. Most of us figured Harvey for a snitch.'

I felt my gut wrench up into a knot. 'Harvey Eckers was your squad leader?'

'Yup. Listen, not to be unkind, but it's Christmas Eve and all and we're just about to sit down to dinner. There's not much more I can tell you.'

'Sure.' I was thinking about Eckers, his flyer in Bennett's office. Horns drawn in dark marker. There was a copy of the *Missoulian* on the kitchen counter, and I picked it up and unfolded the front page, my eyes skimming the article about Eckers. 'Starre,' I said.

'What?'

'The senator,' I told Dupres, 'the one Eckers was snitching for. His name was Starre.'

'That's it, Starre,' Dupres agreed. 'That would have bothered me all night.'

I hung the phone up, took one more hit off the vodka bottle, and screwed the cap on tightly. I'd known for a while I was in over my head, but if Harvey Eckers had been involved in Bennett's death, things were worse than I could have ever imagined. There was an unpleasant picture forming in my mind, of Eckers and his uncle, Kingston Starre. And the picture got worse, till it was ugly, troubling. There was Bennett's plane, the neat cross of it in the white cirque where the mountains cradled Fish Lake. And another jet, a second T-33, perhaps, far overhead. And there was Eckers's face behind the glass, determined, shaded by the storm. In my picture he looked down and saw his friend's plane, its nose jammed up into a drift. He made a circle around the snowy bowl, then another, and then, for some dark reason I had yet to understand, he flew home, claiming he had found nothing.

I stared out Kristof's window at the yards of the houses across the street, at fleecy barbecues and swing sets and lawn chairs. The snow kept falling, a work in progress. Like the pouch a spider might make around a fly: translucent at first, the insect's black wings still visible beneath the loose weave of the silk. Later, the fabric dense as a shroud.

A truck pulled up, Kristof's old Chevy. The door opened and he stepped out, his feet landing in the dry snow, his boots raising a fine spray. The streetlamp outside the window cast a yellowish glow on the neighborhood. The air was hazy, thick with the river's exhalation. Kristof took a step forward, then another. Footprints trailed behind him, round-soled imprints like those of a moon walker. Headlights raked across his body, silhouetted his bundled shape. A human being well protected against the elements.

I looked down the block and watched a Suburban with police markings roll forward, pull up in front of the apartment building, and stop, cutting Kristof off. He turned his face up to the driver's side window, moved his lips, then glanced briefly at the window where I stood. A warning, maybe. Or a tiny act of rebellion, his way of giving me away. I took a step back, turned the light off, then moved forward again.

The Suburban's door was open now and the dome light was on. I could see a man inside. A cowboy hat, thick shoulders: Jeff Riley. He leaned forward and handed Kristof something, reached his long arm out, laid his palm on Kristof's shoulder.

They stood like that for a second, two men wanting the same thing, some kind of confession that had nothing to do with Clay Bennett. Nothing to do with Tina Red Deer or Ivan Popov or Amos's body in the snow. Kristof dipped his head slightly, an intimate gesture, a movement I knew so well, something he would do during sex. He said something to Riley; then they both shook hands and smiled.

I watched Jeff Riley drive away, watched Kristof make his way toward the front steps. And I thought about his body above me, the smell in his hair after sex, the veneer of salt on his skin. What I knew about him. What little he knew about me.

And suddenly I understood that I should not be there. I had brought Popov with me, and Riley, all my perils, dangers I was too much of a coward to warn him of. I had come expecting amnesty, a refuge, something that was not Kristof's to give.

The door opened in the foyer below and I fumbled for my parka, slid my arms into the dead man's coat. I heard the mailbox creak, a first footfall on the stairs. I crossed through the kitchen, moving as quietly as possible in my heavy Sorels, my eyes slowly adjusting to the darkness of the apartment. In Kristof's bedroom I popped the window, swung my right leg out over the sill, then my left. My boots found the slick metal of the fire escape. One rung, then another. The cold collected in my lungs, burned against the back of my throat. I took the last rung and dropped down into the snow.

Across the uneven ice of Rattlesnake Creek, the cedar buildings of the Edgewater Motel sprawled out. I stood in the bushes at the side of the yard for a moment, gathering myself, watching the back-lit figures in the occupied rooms. On the second floor a man stood, naked, brushing a woman's hair in the flickering light of a television. He slipped his arm across her stomach, bent his mouth to her neck. Down at the far end of the breezeway a woman in a beige suit unscrewed the cap from a bottle and poured herself a drink.

I could check in, I thought, become one of them. I could lie on the queen-sized bed, on the garish bedspread that had received so many bodies. I could have a life like their lives, the hours ticking away neatly until death, toothbrushes coupled by the sink, shared towels, children dancing under the sunlit spray of a hose. But this was not who I was, and I knew it.

I looked up at Kristof's apartment, watched the light go on, watched him disappear, reappear in the bedroom. He came to the window and stood looking out into the darkness. I wanted to signal to him. *Down here!* I wanted to shout. But I kept my mouth closed, my arms stiff at my sides. Kristof brought his hands up, slammed the window closed. And suddenly I hated myself for watching, hated the person I'd become. The perversity of surveillance. The cold way in which I could remove myself. The power of it.

# Eighteen

My mother believed that her battles with my father were private. She convinced herself that no one knew, especially not me. She saw herself as a good mother, and I used to think this was the reason she stayed with him: for my sake. Both of them thrived on the struggle, on the other's power and their own weakness. My father's trips to the reservation were just a small skirmish in the larger battle.

Though I heard my parents' fights through the walls of our house, my mother would never have fought in front of me. In the years before the accident, I only saw her angry one time. I was in fourth grade and she came to the doorway of my science classroom and stood outside, waving at me through the glass until the teacher let me go. She had lit a cigarette in the hallway and the smell of it was unnatural there in the school, forbidden.

'I told them you had a doctor's appointment,' she said. 'We're going for a drive.' Then we went outside and got in the car.

I used to love to watch my mother drive, and this day was no different. Her hands were beautiful on the steering wheel, muscular yet graceful. Her skin rode over the small knobs of bone in her wrists, making her seem birdlike, delicate and vulnerable. When she pressed down on the accelerator, the muscles in her legs flexed.

She lit another cigarette and headed across town and up onto the highway. Now that I think about it, it must have been late enough in the fall that the road through Glacier was already snowbound, because we took the long way up to Browning. Straight across the mountains to Helena, then north along the Rocky Mountain Front.

It was a beautiful day when we started: clear autumn light on the Blackfoot River, hay bales like giant loaves of bread. But coming down off Rogers Pass the weather turned nasty. The wind rolled in off the Great Plains, whistling across the side of our station wagon. It never snowed, but there was a constant threat of snow. The clouds were the color of gray flannel, rimmed a dark charcoal. Cattle huddled against one another.

There was a purposefulness to my mother's driving, a sense of something at stake. She only spoke once, when we stopped for gas and cigarettes, and then it was just to ask if I needed to use the bathroom. It was quiet in the car. She kept the radio off, kept the window cracked because of the smoke. I knew she was angry and knew better than to ask where we were going.

We stopped at the Bureau of Indian Affairs office in Browning, and my mother opened her door, swinging her pumps out onto the gravel road. 'Wait here,' she told me.

I watched her go inside, watched the door swing closed behind her. A knapweed-choked field across from the BIA office was littered with rusting carcasses of cars, the insides of washing machines, a couple of lopsided trailers. A man came up to the car, a Blackfeet, his hair gray and wild. He put his face to the driver's window, looked in at me, then wandered over to the field. He pounded hard on the side of one of the trailers. Another man opened the door, looked out, laughed.

I stayed in the car for a good twenty minutes. The two men came out of the trailer, sat on a couple of cinder blocks in the field, and drank beers. When my mother came back, her eyes were pink and swollen. She slid behind the wheel, lit a cigarette, smoothed her hair where it had come out of its clips.

A white man came out of the BIA office and climbed into a truck. My mother started the engine. We followed the truck a few miles out of town. The man pulled off the road, waved once, and my mother turned down a long dirt driveway.

There was a small farmhouse at the end of the driveway, white clapboard with a broad front porch. Because it was fall, the garden was dead, but the brown stalks were tied in neat bundles, the roses trimmed down and mulched with straw. The door of the tidy house opened and my father came out.

My mother cut the engine and stepped from the car. She walked across the lawn, her pumps slightly off-kilter on the uneven ground. Her gray skirt was tight against her thighs. My father stepped off the porch to meet her, and she raised her hand and brought it down hard on his cheek.

Then she hit him again, her fists on his chest this time. He didn't move, just stood there with his arms limp at his sides. She hit him again and again, until he finally took her wrists in his hands and held her away.

I saw my mother's legs buckle beneath her, and my father's palm against her shoulder blade. He walked her back to the car, leaned down, and whispered something in her ear. I looked away, trying to concentrate on anything but them: the white line of the mountains, the rhythm of an oil well in a neighboring field. The door popped open and my mother slid in next to me.

'Hey, kiddo,' my father said.

I thought of that day for several years afterward, the shame of watching them. Sometime in high school I let it go, let the memory tuck itself away.

But when I left Kristof's that night, the trip to Browning came rushing back to me. As I drove west along Broadway, past the Super Six Motel and Clay Bennett's old office on the Clark Fork, I was thinking about my father's mouth bent down to my mother's ear. I was wondering what he might have said to her, what he could have told her to make her get back in the car. It was one of the great mysteries of my life. Whatever it was, she started the engine and rolled forward, headed back down across the plains toward home.

It was just after six when I pulled up in front of Harry Ford's place out in Travois Village. The trailer was swarming with lights: white cascading from the eaves, red and green blinking circles around the windows and door. I was dizzy just looking at it. Old Talking Heads music blared through the front door, and I knocked loudly. Harry's girlfriend, Cherise, answered, her hair strewn with tinsel, a chain of ribbons and bows around her neck. Underneath an old bathrobe her skin was blotched with bright colors.

'Is Harry around?' I asked.

Cherise nodded and led me through the living room to the bedroom. 'He's in here,' she said. 'We're painting. I hope you don't mind.'

I shook my head. Cherise closed the door and Harry turned toward us, smiling. He was naked, cross-legged on the floor, a plastic tarp spread out around him. His Santa suit was draped on the waterbed behind him, the fabric garish and red against a leopard-print spread.

'We're painting,' Harry said happily. He picked a large brush up off the tarp, dipped it into a gallon of fuchsia paint.

Cherise opened her robe and let it fall to the floor. Harry got up and ran the brush along her stomach, down across her pubis. She walked across the room, pressed herself to the wall, and stepped away, proudly examining the mural of smeared handprints and chest prints.

Harry smiled. 'What's up, Meg?'

'I was wondering about your offer,' I said.

Cherise wandered back to the tarp and Harry slapped some green onto her breasts. 'What offer?'

'About going up to Fish Lake.'

'When do you want to go?' he asked.

'You doing anything tomorrow?' I smiled. 'I

know it's Christmas, but I really need to get out there.'

He put his brush down, picked up his pipe, and lit the bowl, taking a long toke. 'As long as it's okay with her,' he said, motioning to Cherise.

She nodded her head, put her hand in a pot of blue paint.

Harry winked at me. 'Can we go early?'

'Sure.'

'How about we meet at seven-thirty, at the airport? That way we'll get up there right around sunrise.'

I was surprised by his willingness, surprised he didn't even ask why I wanted him to fly me up the Bitterroot.

'Okay, then,' he said, putting his hand on Cherise's naked hip, nodding to the Santa suit on the bed. 'Time for me to get dressed.'

I was planning to head downtown after I left Harry and Cherise's. There was a big Christmas Eve potluck at Charlie's bar, and I thought I might hook up with Darwin and go over to the Amvets with her for her show. In the back of my mind I thought I might even get lucky and run into Josie before Popov got to her. I was having regrets about telling the Russian about her, thinking she might be able to answer some questions for me. Like whether Harvey Eckers was paying her for her services.

I was thinking about how I might get her to talk when I hit the traffic lights at Russell Street. I tapped my right blinker and slowed to a stop, then checked my left for cars. And that's when I saw it. It was hard to miss, really, some thirty feet of pink neon screaming in the darkness, and I kicked myself for not having thought of it sooner. LIBERTY LANES, the sign proclaimed, the last letter sputtering and blinking. My mind hurtled back to Amos's trailer, to the strange array of bowling posters, the purple bag and the blue ball.

The light turned green and I leapt across the intersection, my wheels spinning as I made a hard left into the parking lot of Liberty Lanes. I parked by the door and shoved my hand deep in the pocket of my coat, feeling the little key with my fingers, the curl of paper marked LIBERTY. The door of the building was blacked out and dark, but the sign over the entrance read OPEN 24 HOURS. I hopped out of the truck and onto the walkway, Amos's logic suddenly clear to me. There's no safer hiding spot than a public place.

The atmosphere at the bowling alley was less than festive. Only a handful of the lanes were in use. 'Silent Night' drifted from the karaoke bar.

'Can I help you?' The kid at the shoe rental counter put down a bedraggled copy of *The Shining* and squinted at me.

'You guys rent lockers?' I asked.

'Sure.' He shrugged. 'The sales counter's not open today, though. You'll have to come back tomorrow.'

'Where are they?' I smiled.

'The sales counter?' the kid asked dubiously.

'No,' I told him, 'the lockers.'

'Oh.' His skin was shiny under the ceiling lights,

speckled with acne. 'They're back there, around the bar.'

'Thanks,' I said, slipping the key out, reading the number stamped into its head.

One of the bowlers, a cowboy, bowled a strike, sending the pins slamming into one another. Ninety-eight . . . seventy-six . . . fifty-four . . . I counted down the row of metal doors, stopping at forty-six, and slid the key into the lock. It was a perfect fit. I took a deep breath, glanced around the empty alcove, and tugged at the handle, feeling the hinges slide open.

The locker wasn't large, maybe a foot and a half square and two feet deep. Inside were a well-worn pair of bowling shoes and a soft cloth, the kind you'd use to clean your ball. I took the shoes out and set them on the floor. The laces were tied, the tongues tucked neatly inside. Behind the shoes, pushed up against the back of the locker, was a video-cassette. I pulled it out and read the label: DECEMBER 20.

It seemed safe in the bowling alley and I couldn't bring myself to leave. I was exhausted, tired of Tina and Clay Bennett, tired of the Sig in my pocket. Putting the shoes back in the locker, I closed the door and sat down on one of the benches that looked out over the lanes. I needed a VCR, a quiet place to watch the tape, and I thought briefly about going back to Kristof's. I wished I knew what he had said to Jeff Riley, whether he had lied for me, whether he had offered to set me up. I wished I knew what he was thinking when he glanced at me in the window. I wouldn't have blamed him for giving me away. He had put up with more than enough. I lit a cigarette and smoked it slowly, reveling in the warmth and light, the tender chatter of the bowlers, the pins knocking into one another.

Outside, the wind and cold were still lashing the valley. I had to put all my weight against the door to push it open. Snow blew horizontally in the phosphorescent arcs of the streetlamps. Gripping the tape tight in my mittened hand, I cinched the hood of the parka until only my eyes were showing and made for my truck.

The inside of the windshield was glazed with frost. I took my mittens off, scratched at the glass with my fingernails, slid the key into the ignition. The engine kicked halfway over and died in the cold. I pumped the accelerator once, tried again, and heard the sparks take hold.

I swung by Darwin's first, hoping to catch her before she'd left for the night, but her windows were dark and the door was locked. I checked the time and headed back across the railroad tracks toward downtown. It was just closing in on eight and I figured she'd be down at the Amvets by now, getting ready for her show. I found a parking space next to the courthouse and jumped out.

I could hear the party before I even stepped through the door of the Amvets. The drag show hadn't started yet, but the dance floor was jammed. It was a sea of mismatched bodies: natty young men in crisply pressed khakis; middle-aged women in Wranglers and ranch boots; bearded university professors; cowboys, lawyers, doctors, and Harley riders.

Scanning the crowd for Darwin's dark face, I spotted her by the DJ booth. She was a blonde tonight. Platinum hair and a red dress with gold sequins and quivering fringe. Her legs were long and smooth, lean as a racehorse's. A good-looking cowboy shuffled toward her, gyrated his hips, and disappeared behind a group of kids in sunglasses and psychedelic print clothes who looked like they'd be less out of place at a Miami Beach rave.

Sweltering in Bennett's parka, I elbowed my way forward, waving desperately to get Darwin's attention. The cowboy reappeared, dancing with a young Indian kid now, doing a kind of modified disco two-step while the Indian shuffled his feet in a revised version of traditional native dancing. It was like a poster for the New West. Christ, I thought, waving again, why didn't Darwin see me? Then she looked up, raised her gloved hand like royalty, curled her fingers in a lazy greeting, and made her way toward me.

The music was mind-numbing, Annie Lennox's voice cranked up as loud as it could go. I yelled fruitlessly, pointed to the tape, then to my eyes: a pantomime of viewing. Darwin grabbed my hand, hustled me through the crowd, then behind the bar. We stepped through a door into relative quiet.

'Talk to me, baby girl,' she said, pulling a pack of Virginia Slims from her gold-glittered cleavage, propping the filter between her lips.

'I need to watch this,' I said. 'Your place is locked and I don't have my key.'

Darwin lit the cigarette, put a hand on her hip.

'And the reason why you can't watch it at home would be . . . ?'

I shrugged.

She sighed deeply and looked at me as if I were a disobedient child. 'None of your business,' she said under her breath, then, 'Come on, they've got a VCR in the back.'

I followed her into the office. She closed the door behind us, reached her hand out, and took the tape from me. 'Sit down,' she said, motioning to a well-worn couch. She turned the TV on, popped a tape from the VCR, and fed mine into the rectangular mouth. 'You want a beer or something?'

'Sure' – I nodded – 'and a whiskey.'

She pressed PLAY, handed me the remote, and glided out the door.

Though it wasn't quite the last revelation at Galilee, I had to admit there was something prophetic and wonderful about Amos's face postmortem on the twenty-eight-inch screen of the Amvets television. The tracking was off and the volume low, so he flickered there silently at first, his face distorted by bars of static. I adjusted the picture and cranked up the sound. He was talking about Judgment Day and the final battle for the soul of mankind. Something about the city council's bi-cycle/pedestrian board and Satan's minions. I hadn't ever sat through an entire episode of *Anarchy with Amos* before and I suddenly remembered why.

The tape was crude, evidently filmed at the MCAT studios. A table in the foreground was arrayed with all of Amos's props: a Colt Diamond-back revolver, a leather-bound copy of the King

James Bible, a small shrine to Sid Vicious, a wooden crucifix with an anguished Christ draped languidly across it. I hit the FAST FORWARD button, watched Amos's mouth speed up, his movements become jerky.

Darwin came back in and handed me a Rainier and a tumbler of bourbon – enough alcohol to disable an angry grizzly bear.

'What is this?' she asked, propping herself on the arm of the couch.

'That freak Amos Ortenson made it,' I told her. 'It looks like one of his shows.'

'Not anymore,' she said.

I looked back at the screen. The tape had shifted and Amos's face had disappeared, been replaced by a couple. They were naked. Framed by a window. The figures were small, far away, but their actions were unmistakable. The woman was sucking the man's cock, her head pumping ridiculously in fast-forward motion.

Darwin reached for the remote, slowed the tape to PLAY. 'Looks like Amos was working on some independent projects.' She smiled.

The camera zoomed closer so we could see the woman's features: dark eyes, sharp cheeks, blond hair with brown roots. The man pulled away from her, dropped down. They both disappeared beneath the level of the window. The camera shifted again, panning dizzily across the side of a building, searching. Windows, cars, gray asphalt whipped by, out of focus. Then the lens came to rest on another window, and I recognized the setting immediately.

'It's the Super Six!' Darwin exclaimed, echoing my thoughts.

I nodded. 'Amos lived back behind there, in one of the trailers.'

Darwin chuckled. 'You think he was paying his actors scale?'

This new window was darker than the first. The TV was on somewhere in the depths of the room. A figure crossed in front of the window, stopped, and lit a cigarette. The flame illuminated his face. Gray hair cut short and neat, a square jaw: Clayton Bennett. It was the first time I had seen him living, and he looked very different than he had in death. Less powerful, unguarded, exposed.

A woman walked over to him, her hair dark against her face. It was Tina Red Deer. She put her hand on his shoulder for balance, took an offered cigarette, said something. I saw her walk away, saw a flash of daylight as the door opened, then closed, and two figures slipped out. Tina and Elton, gone to get more booze.

Bennett lingered at the window, smoking his cigarette. At one point he looked down, straight into the camera, and for a second I thought he might know it was there. Amos must have thought so too. The lens dipped, went dark for a moment, then panned back to Bennett. The door opened again, briefly dazzling the room with sunlight. Bennett turned, took a step back. A figure approached him, someone close to his height.

The camera jittered, then steadied itself, zoomed tight on the person's face. It was a woman, her neck thick with muscles, her chest marked with the red body of a dragon. Josie. She brought a gloved hand up above Bennett's head. In her fingers was a knife, a long blade that reflected the blue glint of the television.

'Oh, Jesus!' Darwin whispered.

Bennett put his arm up, sloppily trying to defend himself, but it was no use. Josie cut him again and again.

# Nineteen

One of the first jobs I had when I left home was in the ticket booth of the Pleasure Palace, an adult movie theater in Denver. Not one of the best ways to make a living, but not one of the worst either. There was plenty of downtime, and the customers were mostly quiet, undemanding. After the shows were over I would have to go into the theater to pick up any garbage and wipe the seats down. I would sit on my stool in the little booth until I heard the sound fade out; then I would stand by the doors with my trash can and my rag and bottle of ammonia.

I liked to watch the men come out, watch the expressions on their faces. I was young at the time, not even eighteen, and I could tell my presence startled the patrons. They would glance at me, at my hand on the bottle, and they would become deeply embarrassed, self-conscious.

At the theater where I worked, the houselights never came up. It was a courtesy to the customers, my boss explained. A way to keep the fantasy alive. Who wants to look around, he used to say, and see ten other guys jacking off with you? I was supposed to wait to go in and clean, give everyone a chance to clear out before I threw the main light switch.

Every so often, though, I'd catch a couple of lingerers. A solo was never so bad. He would look up blankly, tuck himself away, and shuffle out the door. But two or more stragglers became awkward. The men would cough, rub their eyes, and pretend they'd been asleep. Or they'd suddenly become intensely interested in the carpeting, or panic and head toward the screen, looking for a back way out when there wasn't one. Always, though, there was absolutely nothing said.

A similar hush fell between me and Darwin in the office of the Amvets. Though Amos's tape told me nothing I didn't already suspect, I felt tainted by it, guilty somehow. Neither of us could look at the other. The lens lingered for a moment after Josie left, an eye obsessed with the empty square of the window. Then the television screen was bright with snow. Darwin hit the remote, switched the TV off.

I sat back, lit a cigarette, and took a long sip of the whiskey. I couldn't help thinking about the Pleasure Palace when the lights came on. Damp tissues on the floor. Condoms like rumpled socks. Cigarette butts. Razor blades. Smears of blood that always made me wonder. Now and then a piece of rope or a plastic bag.

Five minutes passed. Another five. Darwin shifted, and the fabric of her gold dress crackled against the couch. 'What are you going to do?' she asked finally.

I shook my head, wishing I had an answer.

*

It was only two short blocks from the Amvets to the police station. I stood at the corner of Ryman and Broadway, watched two cruisers pull out of the police parking lot, and waited for the light to change. I thought about my options, thought about taking the tape to Riley. Now that the answers were beginning to piece themselves together there was suddenly less urgency to everything. I had been right about Tina, and for a moment it seemed as if her innocence was the only thing that mattered, as if it was I who had been absolved, not her.

But I hadn't been pardoned. The pedestrian light changed to WALK and I stepped off the curb, the Sig bumping against my leg. I sauntered along the eastern side of the courthouse, fumbling for my car keys, the videotape tucked into the breast pocket of Bennett's parka.

What I really wanted was sleep, a long drowsy oblivion beneath cotton and down. I let my eyes fall closed and put my hand on the driver's door of the Ford, thinking of the inner contours of my little house, of navigating it in the dark. When I heard the gentle click of metal sliding into metal, I didn't even flinch. I dipped my head slightly, as if laying my neck out to receive the blade, and imagined the mechanism of the gun next to my face, the hammer cocked to fire, the bullet like a shiny pill.

I opened my eyes and looked up, saw Josie at the other end of the barrel. Her arm was rigid, an extension of the gun she was holding. Her face was twisted, angry. She was propped on one hip, her legs sprawled out in the bed of my Ford, her stomach strong and tight.

'Put your hands on your head,' she said, swinging one foot over the side of the truck's bed and hopping down onto the pavement. 'Now walk around to the passenger door.'

I nodded.

Josie shadowed my face, keeping the gun pressed to the side of my cheek. 'Open the door,' she said when we rounded the truck, 'and get in. Put your hands on the dashboard and slide over.'

There was something jumpy and unpredictable about her that made me do as I was told. I positioned myself behind the wheel while Josie climbed into the passenger seat and closed the door.

'Put the key in the ignition and drive,' she told me.

'Where are we going?' I asked.

She settled in beside me, her gun aimed at my side. 'Just drive.' She grunted, nodding toward Broadway. 'I'll tell you where when you need to know.'

The streets of downtown were deserted but the bars were all open. At Front Street we cruised east, then turned onto the Higgins Avenue bridge. The river beneath us was still frozen solid. Near the far bank, where the bed wound into a deep curve, a few ribbons of black water bubbled up from under the milky ice. To the west I could just barely make out the beams and girders of the Orange Street bridge. Beyond it, invisible, was the no-man's-land of the defunct paper mill and the rocky island where Tina and Elton had taken the body of Clay Bennett.

'Must've been a real lucky break with those Indians,' I said. 'I can't imagine you could have planned it any better.'

Josie didn't say anything. She shifted, pulling a cigarette from the pocket of her leather coat.

I kept one eye on her lap, on the weapon hovering there. It was a Taurus Raging Bull, the same kind of gun I'd seen at Hop's pawnshop. The revolver was so big it dwarfed her, made her look like Yosemite Sam minus the mustache. It was a strange choice of weaponry, more powerful than necessary.

'What's that shoot?' I asked.

She shrugged. We'd reached the South Hills and she jerked her head to the left. I nosed the Ford up past the old quarry, up into the dark folds of Pattee Canyon. There had been a large fire in the ravine when I was a child. Now a bald patch ran for miles up the flanks of the mountain. We crossed stump-stubbled fields dotted with snow-ghosted mock orange and chokecherries and baby pines. A herd of mule deer scattered in the beam of my headlights, their hooves kicking loose snow.

We passed out of the burn into dense woods and kept on climbing. The asphalt petered to gravel. I looked at Josie for directions. Her jaw was set hard, gilded by the lights of the dash panel.

'Keep going,' she told me.

Five minutes up the dirt road she poked me in the ribs with the Taurus. 'Here.'

I pulled the truck to a stop and shifted into park,

leaving the engine running. 'Get out,' she said, popping her door, grabbing me around the waist, pulling me roughly toward her. 'This way.'

I thought about the Sig in my pocket, thought about going for it in the commotion, then figured I'd have a better chance out in the open.

It was freezing outside the truck, but not as cold as down in the valley. Up here in the woods there was little wind. We were just above the Deer Creek drainage, high up on the back of Mount Sentinel. My headlights tunneled out into the snowy undergrowth. The right side of the road dropped off suddenly, swooping down toward the river and East Missoula.

'The first time I talked to you, I tried to be nice,' Josie said. 'But my patience is running out.' She grabbed my right arm and twisted it hard behind my back. Tears stung my eyes. 'Where's the map?'

I breathed deeply, trying to calm myself. I needed a plan, some way out, if I didn't want to end up like the others. I thought about my Sig, Josie's Taurus, the honed steel of a knife somewhere beneath her coat.

One of the first lessons you learn about weaponry is that what you choose to carry depends very much on the situation in which you are planning to use it. Sometimes the choice is easy, based on the simplest of logic: You don't go squirrel hunting with an Uzi, unless what you're after is squirrel hamburger. Sometimes the variables are subtler, like noise or force of kick or size of cartridge. Take the Sig, for instance. It's a solid all-purpose gun, easy to handle and good for situations where you need to keep things quiet, but it lacks the power and stamina of the big boys. Poor Josie, I thought, she's going to learn this crucial lesson the hard way.

As guns go, the Raging Bull is more specifically engineered than most. You might use it for elk hunting or to ward off grizzlies and it would sure look good on film, but it's not really a working gun, it's more for show. It's impressive as hell, though, and I could see why Josie had chosen it.

'What are you hoping to find out there,' I asked, 'in Bennett's plane?'

I felt her hand twitch. She shifted the butt in her palm and the barrel jumped on my side. The Taurus had to weigh at least four pounds, and I figured her wrist was starting to ache. I took another deep breath and kicked her hard in the shins. She loosed her grip, giving me a second of freedom, and I took it. Spinning around, I brought my right leg up with as much force as I could muster and kneed her in the groin.

She doubled over, the Taurus sliding up toward my face. I threw a right hook, felt my knuckles connect with her jaw. Josie reeled back, the weight of the huge gun pulling her off kilter. In the time it took her to regain her balance I'd found the butt of my Sig with my fingers. I stepped forward and jammed the barrel into the fleshy part of her neck, just below her ear.

'Nice gun,' I told her. 'Mind if I have a look?' I ran my left hand down her arm and pried the monster revolver from her fingers. 'You know, I prefer an automatic myself.'

She looked at me and winced. Her breath hung nearly solid in the still air.

When I lived down in Miami, my boyfriend had a business association with a guy named Luther Thompson who raised alligators out off the Tamiami Trail. Luther supplemented his income by making late-night runs in his airboat, collecting cargo that had been dropped in the Everglades. My friend was in distribution, and every couple of weeks we'd make a trip out to Luther's farm to pick up merchandise.

Luther was a mean man, meaner than anyone I'd met up until then. During the day he wrestled alligators at the farm, charging tourists big money to watch the shows. He kept his wrestling partners well fed and sluggish. Before the shows he and his son would go back to the pens, bind the animals' jaw shut, and shoot them full of tranquilizers. Then, just for good measure, they'd taunt the gators, letting them thrash around in the mud pit until they were crippled with exhaustion. It was never a fair fight.

I remember that when Luther won – and he always won – he would strut around the pen with his hands over his head and his gut thrust out above his muddy jeans.

There in the woods high above Deer Creek, looking down at the top of Josie's head, I was reminded of Luther's alligators and of the strange mix of revulsion and pity they stirred up in me. And I loathed myself. My own capacity for violence disgusted me: the things I had done to get by, what I was about to do.

I had forced Josie to her knees, down on the crusted snow. I could hear her shivering, the chatter of her teeth. Pressing the Sig to the back of her neck, I held the Taurus out in front of her. 'Poor choice of weaponry,' I said. I bent down and set the revolver on the snowy ground behind me, well out of her reach. 'Now the Sig-Sauer, that's a nice execution gun. For one thing it's neat. Won't get me dirty, you know.'

She wrenched her neck, turned her face up to me. I could smell the fear on her, a clean smell like the inside of a hospital, like ammonia.

'You think *your* patience is running out?' I asked her. 'Talk to me, Josie. Here's your chance to save a life. I know you're working for Harvey Eckers. What's out there in the Bitterroots?'

I brought the Sig up and hit her hard across the back of her neck. Her throat wrenched upward. She doubled over, gagging, and vomited onto the snow. Her hands were bare, the fingers bright from the cold. She moved her hand toward the inside of her jacket and I slapped it away, grabbed a fistful of her hair.

'You're hired help,' I reminded her. 'Look around. Did he pay you enough for it all to end right here?'

Josie raised her head slightly, her eyes scanning the woods. The headlights hit her right across the face. She was older than I'd thought, her skin riddled with fine lines.

'I don't know what's out there,' she said, her voice dry, hoarse. 'And I'm not working for Eckers. At least he's not the one paying me.'

'Open your coat,' I told her, the barrel of the Sig tight against her temple. 'Slowly.'

She reached down and unzipped her jacket, opening one side, then the other. I reached into the left breast pocket and pulled out a bone-handled knife.

'Who's paying you?' I asked.

I put the knife in my pocket, undid my belt with my free hand, and slid it from the loops of my jeans.

'Put your hands behind your back,' I told Josie.

I fastened the belt around her wrists and pulled the leather tight.

'Who's paying you?' I repeated.

'Some fruit company,' she said. Her breath had frozen and collected in her hair, turning it white around her face.

'What's their name?' I asked, but I already knew the answer. Star Fruit, Starry Fruit. That's what Gloria had said. But it was Starre Fruit, as in Kingston Starre. Bennett had worked for them before the crash. No doubt the checks he'd been getting weren't part of a pension plan.

'Starre Fruit,' Josie answered. I pulled her wrists and she struggled up off her knees.

'Did you kill Ivan?' I asked as we left the interstate and headed north on Highway 93. I was sure of it, but I needed to hear the answer from Josie.

She slumped against the door of the truck, her shoulders wrenched to one side. 'Yes.' She grunted. 'It was my job.'

'And Amos?'

She rolled her eyes toward me, narrowed her lids

until the whites were just two tiny sparks. 'He was stupid. He wanted money.'

We were silent for the rest of the trip to Hot Springs. It was late and there was almost no one on the road. I drove fast, keeping my eyes on the bright arc of my headlights, watching for deer. Josie never once asked where we were going. After Ravalli she fell asleep, her cheek to the cold glass. More than once I thought about turning back. I knew what Nick would do to her, and I had to keep reminding myself of the way Amos had looked in the snow and of the picture she'd taken of Kristof, what she would have done to him.

It was moving on into the early hours of the morning when I took the turnoff into Hot Springs and found the old church. I banged hard on the front door and watched a light flicker in an upstairs bedroom.

'Get out,' I told Josie. She climbed down onto the driveway, and I got in the truck and pulled away. In my rearview mirror I watched the door open, saw the flaps of Nick Popov's white bathrobe as he stepped outside to meet her.

# Twenty

The Missoula International Airport, international only because of one or two prop planes that fly in from Canada each day, sits in the western flatlands of the valley. Wind-scoured and as yet still unscarred by the creeping sprawl of subdivisions, it's a lonely stretch of land. To the north lie the railroad tracks; eastward, along the rails, are warehouses and the stockyards.

Christmas morning was unusually clear. The thermometer was still way below zero, keeping the valley in a frigid coma. Hoarfrost had settled on trees and on the eaves of buildings. From the tarmac behind the private-aviation hangar I could see the entire bleak icescape of the valley, the hills like frozen waves on an arctic sea, the snow-dredged mountains that separated the lights of town from the dark folds of the wilderness. To the west, the paper mill glittered like a futuristic fairy castle.

It was early morning when I'd gotten back from Hot Springs. I tried for a couple of hours of sleep in the parking lot of the truck stop at the Y, but it was too cold for comfort and I'd ended up inside drinking weak coffee. Now I was high on lack of sleep. I shuffled from one foot to the other and rubbed my palms together like I was trying to start a fire.

'Nineteen below,' Harry Ford remarked happily, tapping at a small thermometer that dangled from the zipper of his parka. 'Looks like we're coming out of this cold snap.'

I nodded, shivering, and knocked the heels of my Sorels together, trying to drum up some body heat.

'Merry Christmas,' Harry said, sliding a small pipe out of his pocket and taking a hit. 'You ever been in one of these?' He popped the door of the Sikorsky and motioned for me to get in the other side.

'No,' I told him.

He smiled like he had a secret and chuckled gleefully. When we climbed inside he handed me an empty Fritos bag, saying, 'Hold on to this.'

We headed northwest, the helicopter swaying in the wind like a baby's cradle. Over Squaw Peak, Harry turned the Sikorsky into a tight bank and shot straight south across the valley. I felt the first sinking twinge of nausea in my gut. A few minutes later, when Harry tore open a package of Ho Hos and offered one to me, I doubled over with my mouth to the Fritos bag and regurgitated my coffee.

'You want to go back?' he yelled, spitting chocolate crumbs.

I shook my head no, then pressed my forehead to the window and watched the sparse lights along the highway disappear beneath the body of the helicopter. Beyond the scattered settlements there was nothing but blackness, miles of roadless government land.

'Don't worry,' Harry shouted, 'we'll have light by the time we get up there. See?' He tapped the window next to him with his thumb. 'Sun's already coming up!'

Beyond his chest a bright strip of blue had appeared over the horizon.

'Fish Lake, right?' he shouted, stuffing another Ho Ho into his mouth. The noise in the helicopter was deafening. I could barely hear him. 'You gonna tell me what you're looking for?'

'An old plane!' I yelled, leaning forward against the seat belt, peering out the nose. Everything, the sky and the land and the few high clouds, was the same shade of blue, a color I couldn't quite name, like indigo or the back-lit blue of stained glass.

Harry reached into his parka and pulled his pipe out. He took his hand off the controls momentarily to light the bowl, and the Sikorsky plunged precariously downward. My stomach reeled again.

'You talking about Clay Bennett's T-Thirty-three?' he asked.

'You know about it?'

'Hell, we all knew about it. Clay's been coming up here every summer since I can remember to look for the damn thing. When he moved to Missoula and started the charter business, he made a point of telling every pilot in the area to keep an eye out. That season back a few years ago when we had all those fires up the Bitterroot, Clay would be on me every time he saw me. It was a sad story, really. Seems like he'd decided to pack it in, though.'

'You mean by selling his plane?'

Harry nodded. 'To tell you the truth, I'm not all that surprised, his giving up the search. It's not a cheap project. Fuel alone runs you a fortune, and this fall Clay was flying out almost every day. Probably broke him in the end.'

I passed him one of the Ho Hos and thought about Bennett's debts, the unpaid bills in his office. He must have been putting everything he had into the search, planning to clear out of town when it was over. 'I think he found the plane,' I said.

Harry smiled, satisfied. 'About time, I guess. I could sympathize, you know? You sure you don't want one?' he asked, fingering the chocolate cake.

'No, thanks. He ever tell you why he was so anxious to find that old jet?'

Harry shook his head.

I looked down at the snowscape and thought about Bennett struggling through the dark hills. 'I heard he walked out,' I said.

'What?'

'I guess he walked!' I yelled.

Harry nodded. 'He found some fire lookout and waited out the thaw; wouldn't have survived otherwise. It was early spring when he went down, too snowy to walk out.'

He stuffed the entire Ho Ho into his mouth and chewed thoughtfully.

'I ran into him one night out at the Forest Lounge. He gets a couple of drinks in him and starts telling me about that month he spent at the lookout. The place is full of books, I guess. Books

and a cupboard full of canned beans. So he rips
these books up for kindling.'

Harry stopped, shook his head in amazement.

'Guy survives two months out here and all he can
talk about is these fucking books, how he tore the
endings out, or the beginnings, how he had to read
these books with missing pages. I guess he was kind
of nuts, you know?'

'What books?' I asked, like an onlooker at a car
wreck, curious for the details.

'Oh, every kind, I guess. Cookbooks, astronomy
books, romance stories, Westerns. There's not
much to do up at those lookouts 'cept read.'

The chopper nosed upward, skimming the top of
a high ridge. The ground rushed up to meet us, then
fell away. For a moment we were so close to the
trees that the draft from our rotors kicked snow off
the boughs of the pines.

'I don't understand why it took him so long to
find the plane,' I said, feeling my stomach catch in
my throat. 'He said he landed at that airstrip,
right?'

Harry laughed. 'Look down there. You really
think he knew for sure where he was? Plus from
what I hear it was storming like a motherfucker
when he went down.'

He was right and I knew it. The mountains
below were monotonous and uniform, each ridge
and gully like the next. To the east I could just see
the first warm tip of the sun, the orange ribbon of it
bright as a bloodstained yolk. The light had
changed from blue to rosy pink, and the snowy
land with it.

'Here we are,' Harry proclaimed.

The Sikorsky dropped quickly, tilting over the peak of Freezeout Mountain and into the bowl of a snowy cirque.

'Where?' I asked, searching the landscape. Below us stretched a long flat field, the surface of the snow blown smooth as a mirror.

Harry turned again, made a tight loop, and parked the Sikorsky in a hover.

'The landing strip,' I said proudly, looking across the treeless meadow. 'But where's the lake?'

Harry smiled grimly. 'I'll be damned!' He whistled. 'That is the lake.' Then he turned the chopper 90 degrees and pointed to a narrow swath that had been cut through the trees. 'Over there's the landing strip.'

Suddenly Bennett's mistake was obvious, the same mistake I had made. Of course he couldn't have seen it in summertime. The lake and the crude runway were almost the same size and shape. With the water frozen and covered in snow, it was nearly impossible to tell which was which. Both were just treeless clearings. I thought about the succession of maps, how they had all been marked with warm-weather dates – all except for the last one. And the northward-pointing arrow he'd drawn, as if trying to confirm the exact nature of his confusion. In the end, when he finally saw the lake under snow, he must have realized what he had done; how, all those years ago, he had nosed the T-33 onto the ice.

'I guess he was close,' I said.

Harry looked at me, serious. 'You know what

they say. Close don't count except in horseshoes and hand grenades. Now we know why they never found the plane. If he put her down on the ice, she would've sunk like a stone when the thaw came.'

We took a different route back to Missoula, skating over the same terrain Bennett must have hiked all those years ago, coming out of the mountains over Hamilton, then heading due north. We passed the Blodgett Creek drainage with its towering crags and sheer walls, then skimmed the mouths of Mill and Sweathouse creeks. Peering back into the deep interiors of the drainages, I couldn't help but wonder which one Bennett emerged from.

After he found the fire lookout and after the snow melted, it would have been relatively easy to find a way out. The Selway-Bitterroot Wilderness Area is a tangled web of trails. It would have only been a matter of time before he found his way along one of them to civilization.

I imagined the first faces he saw, two fishermen tying their hoppers for a hopeful dance over the surface of the creek. I imagined the two bewildered men taking him over to the local café for steak and eggs and a great slab of rhubarb pie. And for some reason I imagined him going home with all those unfinished books in his head: a pair of lovers halfway through disrobing left to dangle in the void created by the missing pages; a recipe for elk stew with a list of ingredients but no directions.

Did the woman in the romance cross the room and press her back into the rich velvet of the settee, he might have thought, or did they simply make love where they stood, the man propping the woman's thighs against the narrow ledge of the windowsill? Was there a pattern on the bedsheets: birds in flight, washed-out purple flowers? Were the linens white like an eggshell under the quilted duvet? Did the cowboy in the Western finally kill the Indian? Or did the Comanches creep into town in the dark of night and slit everyone's throats? And what about the girl in the red dress? How did she come into the story in the first place?

The thaw must have come quickly. What had George Dupres said about the weather? Changeable. First the snow fell, the soft cloak of it settling on the plane, making it invisible; then the melt. I imagined the first warm day and the ice groaning and buckling under the weight. Soon after, maybe the next afternoon, under the force of brilliant sunshine, hairline fissures appeared. By sunset the ice softened and the plane ripped through the frangible surface, bobbing for a while, perhaps minutes, perhaps an hour or more, then sinking into the black water.

What a surprise it must have been to Bennett, the disappearance of this great machine he thought he had set down on solid ground. What a shock to see the lake's treachery.

In the end, Bennett's mistake must have seemed remarkably clear to him. He must have seen what we saw, the long empty snowfield of Fish Lake and the smaller strip of the airfield beside it. In a way, this realization would have been a revival of faith, a reconfirmation of Bennett's judgment, of his ability to navigate. Like when you finally find your car keys, jammed in the kitchen drawer where you left them for safekeeping.

'Harry?' I yelled. 'What do you know about Kingston Starre?'

'Him personally or his family?'

'Both,' I said.

'I'd say he's just a major asshole. You grow up that rich, I guess it's bound to happen.'

'What about Starre Fruit? That's his family's company, right?'

Harry nodded. 'Didn't they teach you anything in history class?'

I shrugged, shook my head.

'Starre Fruit practically owns the Western Hemisphere. Think about it. They sure aren't growing pineapples in Washington State. You don't hear much about them anymore, but back in the fifties and sixties they were a major player. If it weren't for them, Castro wouldn't have had much of a fight on his hands. Money and guns, it all came from Starre Fruit.'

'Why did they care about politics?'

Harry looked at me in disbelief. 'Money, property. The first thing the socialists did was to nationalize private lands. Starre Fruit funded every right-wing government south of the border – well, Starre and the CIA, but for a long time it was hard to say which was which.'

Money and guns, I thought, valuable cargo. Suddenly the gnarl of questions began to untangle for me. Had Bennett known what he was carrying that day? He must have. He'd been getting money from Starre and must have carried similar cargo many times. As his squad leader, Eckers could have arranged everything. Training flights. Training planes. I thought of the pictures in Bennett's office, the long sandy beach, a rippling field of sugarcane.

And what about the canceled search? Had they sacrificed Bennett, thinking they'd come back later for the plane – Eckers and Starre and whoever else was involved – not knowing it would be gone with the first warm day? I thought about what Harry had said. Starre and the CIA, but for a long time it was hard to say which was which. It wouldn't have looked good, an Air Force plane full of guns and money. There would have been questions. All these years they'd been paying him to keep quiet, and all these years he'd been looking for what he knew was still in that plane.

And then what? Had he told them he'd found it and they'd sent someone to kill him out of greed? Out of fear that Eckers's past would be dredged up during an election year? I doubted I would ever know for certain what had happened, but I had a pretty good idea.

It was midmorning by the time we passed Stevensville and the bald dome of St. Mary's Peak. At Lolo the river below us widened, winking and shimmering in the sudden daylight. A Rail Link train, its cars laden with coal, charged along the tracks toward Missoula. Wood smoke curled up out of chimneys.

For an instant I couldn't help thinking of my parents, thinking of the planking of love pulled out from under them in the same way the ice of Fish Lake had broken that day. But isn't that what love is, really? A deception, like the hard pack of snow on ice, a chasm toward which you fall and fall, a place of constant uncertainty?

Harry and I were quiet for the rest of the flight. When the Sikorsky settled onto the tarmac and I climbed out, it took a moment for my legs to adjust to steady ground. After the roar of the chopper, the natural silence of the world seemed extraordinary.

# Twenty-One

I left Harry at the airport and headed home. I was exhausted; all I could think of was sleep. It was Christmas morning and Missoula was as quiet as I'd ever seen it. The twenty-four-hour Safeway was closed. Even the crazy street preacher who normally hung out on the corner of Broadway and Higgins had taken the day off.

My little house seemed changed, in the same way a lover seems different after a long time away, his body unfamiliar in your hands. I undressed and stood under the hot shower, listening to the water hitting the tub, the whine of pressure in the pipes. It took me a good half hour to warm myself; then I padded through the dark house and slipped into bed, still thinking about the plane sinking downward, the instant when the melting ice gave way and the aircraft relinquished its weight. Then there would have been silence again, and the gash of the open water, black against the white bowl of the snowy cirque.

It was late afternoon and already dark when I woke. Artificial light glared through the chinks in the curtains, lay in neat lines on the carpet. Where the light fell there was movement, shadows like feathers rushing downward, like a cascade of water on a clear pane. I sat up, swung my legs off the bed, walked to the window, and pushed the curtains aside. Harry Ford had been right. It had warmed considerably, enough for it to snow.

I threw my robe on and stepped outside onto the porch. After the days of relentless cold, the air seemed wondrously mild. Plush flakes clung to the hoods of cars, to streetlamps.

Headlights rounded the corner of the Dairy Queen, and I recognized Kristof's truck. He pulled up to my curb, cut the engine, and got out. I watched his face as he crossed the yard, his delicate forehead, the slope of his nose.

'Meg!' he called. 'Jesus, what's wrong with you? Where have you been?'

He faltered on the slick steps and I reached out, catching him before he slipped.

'You didn't even bother closing the window, you know?' he said, regaining his balance, stepping up onto the porch.

'What did Chief Riley have to say?' I sneered.

Kristof's head was bare. The snow collected on his brown hair like a wool cap. A flake fell into his eye, lodged itself on his lashes. 'He wanted to know where you were two nights ago.'

'What did you tell him?' I asked.

'I told him you were with me. That we met up at Al and Vic's and spent the afternoon and evening together; then you stayed the night.'

'You lied,' I said simply.

Kristof tilted his head, as if seeing me from a

different angle might help him understand. 'I know.'

I opened my mouth to speak, hesitated a moment. 'Don't you even want to know?'

'Know what?'

'If I killed him?'

Kristof shook his head. I was astounded by his faith, ashamed at what I thought he had done.

'You need to go,' I said coldly. 'It's over.'

'Christ, Meg,' he muttered, putting his hands to his face, like a man trying to defend himself. His mouth opened slightly and I was certain I knew the words he was forming. Love, I thought, but he didn't say anything. He turned and started back down the walk, the wet snow clinging to his boots.

I knew this would be the last time he would go, the last misunderstanding between us. I also knew I could stop him if I wanted to. I could ask him to come inside and we could climb into bed together. I knew how he would smell, exactly which motions he would make, which sounds. But I let him go. It was the only good thing I had done in a long time, and I was proud of myself, of the generosity of the gesture. Kristof's truck sputtered into first gear; he shifted upward and drove away.

I went inside, started a pot of coffee, and put some soup in the microwave. I was at the kitchen table when I heard the knock on my front door, and at first I stayed put. If it was Kristof I wasn't sure I'd be able to turn him away a second time. The visitor knocked again, louder, and I heard whoever it was fumbling with the doorknob, the lock clicking. I got up and ducked around the kitchen doorjamb. I could see Nick Popov's goon, Gregor, his face bright under the porch light. He pounded on the glass again. I crossed through the living room and opened the front door.

Gregor stepped around me and inside. He had a beautiful Wilson Combat in his right hand, a forty-five auto with a silencer. 'Hello, Meg,' he said. 'You will please to get dressed and come with me, yes?' It wasn't a question.

I stared down at his gun, my feet refusing to move.

The Russian put his left hand gently on my elbow. 'It is a simple request,' he told me.

I nodded and went into the bedroom.

It was a long ride up to Hot Springs. At least that's where I assumed we were headed. My escort had about as much to say as the early Arnold Schwarzenegger in *Conan the Barbarian*. I was nervous and tried asking questions in the car, like where we were going and why. When we passed the turnoff to Paradise, Gregor pulled to the shoulder of the road.

'Shut up,' he told me, 'or I will kill you.'

As he'd pointed out earlier, it was a simple request. I kept quiet until we got to Hot Springs, preparing myself for the worst.

It might have been the mood I was in, but the town seemed even more dismal than usual. Even the Christmas lights were cheerless, as if someone official had had the idea that a community decorating effort would be a good idea but no one had quite known how to go through with the plan. The convenience store on the highway blinked like a cheap sex shop. Mismatched garlands and light strings swayed frenetically in the wind along Main Street. A man, a woman, and two young kids cruised by us on their John Deere tractor and pulled up in front of the Pioneer Bar.

If I have to die, I thought, at least let them take me out to Camas Prairie or up into the hills. I couldn't bear the thought of spending my last few moments in Hot Springs.

We drove to Popov's place and pulled around the back. Gregor honked once and Nick came out of the back door of the old church.

'Wait here,' Gregor told me. He and Popov disappeared into a shed and came out moments later with a coil of rope and a couple of cinder blocks. They put the rope and the blocks into the bed of an old GMC truck; then Gregor came over, knocked on my window, and motioned for me to get out. The three of us slid into the cab of the GMC. Gregor had a brief exchange with Nick in Russian, and we were off again, looping through a neighborhood of deserted houses, roofless brick shells sunken in on themselves like the collapsing faces of old men. A sign in the front yard of a still-inhabited shack advertised spa treatments. HERBOLOGY, REFLEXOLOGY, AROMATHERAPY, the sign proclaimed. At a brown block of tribal housing we turned right and headed down a hill.

'Where are we going?' I asked.

Gregor put his gloved hand on the dashboard and flexed it, as if trying to muster up every last bit of self-control. The muscle in his cheek pulsed in and out. He had put the Wilson in his coat, but I could see its bulge against his chest as he drove, like a cold metal heart that had grown on the outside. At the ugly cinder-block community center, Gregor slowed and turned again.

Out of the left-hand window of the truck I could see the pools of the hot springs, two clouds of sulfurous steam rising into the cold air, the mist feathering and whirling away in the wind. Next to the pools, surrounded by a grove of bare-limbed cottonwoods, sat the old bathhouse. It was a large structure, with a thick chimney that made me think of a crematorium. The windows on the second floor were broken and ragged. Tile walls and old pipes like elaborate torture devices were visible inside.

'We are going to the river,' Nick Popov said. Gregor turned back onto the highway, heading south.

The moon was up full and clear by the time we topped the hill and started down into Camas Prairie. Great white clouds of snow hovered over the Buffalo Bill Divide, like silt stirred from a river bottom. The valley was quiet as the grave. Snow stood in sharp peaks like sugary meringue. At the old schoolhouse we turned onto a ranch road and headed up into the Salish Mountains.

The last fifteen miles of the trip were agonizingly slow. The road had evidently been plowed to allow feed trucks to get through, but the old GMC had to labor through several inches of fresh snow. Twice, Gregor and I had to get out and push. Both times I thought briefly about running, considered the prospect of freezing to death, and decided to take my chances with the Russians. Though I was now certain they were going to kill me. I could think of no other reason for our trip out here.

We came upon the Flathead River suddenly. In fact, you could say the river came upon us. The high ground fell away from the arc of our headlights and the Flathead twisted far below like a great black snake. There was just the narrowest line where the river remained unfrozen. I could see the moon in it, a bright coin against the inky ribbon of water, a flicker like a single silver scale. Gregor pulled to a stop, and we all stepped out into a field of snowy sage.

I closed my eyes, took a deep breath of the herb-scented air, and thought of the Flathead, the water green and cold like a jewel, the riffles on the river's surface fluttering like white lace. I imagined my own body beneath it, hair teasing in the current, mouth a home for river eels. More than anything, it was the cold that bothered me, the thought of the perpetual chill. My right knee buckled slightly and I took a tiny step forward, steadying myself. Nick put his hand on my arm, and I flinched from his touch.

'No,' he said, distressed, suddenly understanding. 'No, Meg. You are only to help us.'

Think of your neck stretched out across the cradle of a guillotine, your skin on the worn wood. Think of the blade sliding effortlessly downward on its greased rails. Now imagine some miracle of intervention, a rusty gear, a broken hinge, and the blade jerking to a stop just inches above your spine. Picture it hanging there, the steel glinting while you get up and wander away.

I took a deep breath and looked into Popov's face. He slid a pack of Russian cigarettes from his coat pocket and offered me one. They were thick and black, with shiny gold filters. It was a beautiful night, all blemishes erased by the fresh snow. From where we stood on the high cliff we could see the Moiese Hills and the sparse lights of Round Butte, the vacant land of the Flathead Indian Reservation like part of a pancake that had fallen away.

Gregor popped the truck's back hatch. I could see a shapeless figure in the bed, a body wrapped in a leopard print sheet. *Jesus,* I thought, my stomach turning, it's Josie. *This is what they've done to her – what I've done to her.* Gregor wrestled the body out of the truck and carefully lashed the cinder blocks to the corpse's head and ankles. He came over and stood next to us, nodded to Popov. The dead are heavier and more unwieldy than you expect them to be. It took all three of us to lift Josie up and wrestle her to the eroding side of the cliff.

'I don't know about this,' Nick remarked skeptically, craning his neck forward, surveying the pearly cortex of ice on the river.

Gregor let go of Josie and stepped to the edge. 'It is okay,' he said, with the easy confidence of someone who has done this kind of thing before. He retook his place at Josie's side. 'We will count to three.'

I was surprised by how easily she went over. I was worried she would hit the cliff and bounce, but she sailed right down through the cold air like an osprey rocketing toward a fish. Her back hit the milky ice with a smack and for a moment I thought Nick was right. I thought she might stay there till spring. Then a loud crack echoed up to us, the crust split under her weight, and the orange and black stripes of the sheet disappeared beneath the surface of the Flathead.

'It is deep here,' Gregor commented, wiping his hands on his coat.

Nick Popov looked down at the dark incision, at the water bubbling beneath it. 'I should have left Ivan at home with his mother,' he said sadly.

It was a great relief to get back into the truck, to feel the load lightened. Not because Josie was gone, not because I knew I would live, though these things were not unimportant. The relief came when I understood why Popov had brought me with him. We had made the ultimate business transaction. He had this on me, just as I had something on him. I had become a permanent partner in his guilt.

Our wheels caught for a moment in the deep snow; then the tires found traction and we leapt forward, heading back to Camas.

I looked over at Nick. 'What was it exactly? What had Bennett promised him?'

Nick pulled the collar of his coat tight around his neck, leaned forward, and cranked the heater up another notch. 'Weapons,' he said, finally. He pronounced the *w* like a *v*.

'So the deal was, he helped Clay out with cash flow and when they found what they were looking for they would split the goodies?'

Popov nodded. 'He could have made a lot of money, if he had known what he was doing.' He waved his hand dismissively, as if to say this was the last word on the subject of Ivan and Bennett.

Gregor drove us back to Missoula, his big body hunched over the wheel. None of us said anything till we reached the slow downward grade of Evaro Hill. Then Nick looked over at me.

'Poor woman,' he said, nodding his head to the back of the truck as if Josie were still with us. 'She was only doing her job. We found her quite helpful in the end, full of information, quick with the names of those who hired her. We are not finished yet.'

A semi cruised toward us, its headlights flashing in Nick's eyes. He glanced at Gregor and sighed.

'You know there is such a problem now with people like my son. So greedy for money they forget to think. We have a word for these young Russians who will do anything. It is a Russian word. It means frostbitten.'

I nodded and lit one of my cigarettes. I could see the orange glow of Missoula up ahead of us, the lights of the city radiating off the mountains.

Nick drummed his fingers on the back of Gregor's seat, his eyes hard on my face. 'I wish I had a daughter,' he said.

# Twenty-Two

If the truth be told, I'm a skeptic at heart. I've seen too much of the nastier side of human nature to believe in happy endings. I put little stock in justice and fair play. So I wasn't surprised when this story ended badly. Too many bodies. Too much damage. And in the end it seemed like there was little justice, like all the wrong people had been made to pay. And for what?

When I was a kid we used to camp out in a tent in the backyard of my friend Beth's house and tell ghost stories. There was one about a man who'd murdered his wife and a bloody spot on the bedroom carpet that couldn't be scrubbed away. Another involved a Ouija board that couldn't be destroyed or thrown away. It would spell out the word *die*, over and over again, and there was nothing the owner could do. The board leapt from a hot fire, found its way home from the garbage dump, broke the blade of a hatchet.

This was how I pictured Eckers and Starre in the end: two men sagging under the weight of secrets that would never go away. There was a part of me that pitied them, pitied the relentless progress of their history. These betrayals they could never really rid themselves of. And in a way this was justice, though not nearly what they deserved.

Gregor drove me back to Missoula, across the Higgins Avenue bridge to my house. The temperature was still rising, and steam hung in the cottonwoods along the Clark Fork. The ice had begun to break up. The water was turning viscous, like half-set Jell-O. There was nowhere left for me to go but home.

The new snow on the old pack of ice had made the roads slippery. We fishtailed coming off the bridge. I felt the wheels knock the curb, then right themselves, and I thought about Tina. Something about her had terrified me, the prospect of savagery. More than anything I know, I was afraid she had done the killing. I was afraid of my own capacity for violence, a sisterhood of anger. I wanted to understand the unsolved riddle of her suicide, the misconceptions and despair that had brought her to that last act of self-erasure. But in a way that was the problem, a failure of imagination on my part, an inability to understand. Innocent people don't take their lives, Riley had reasoned. And perhaps she had seen herself for so long in the mirror of eyes like mine and Riley's that she hadn't thought herself innocent anymore.

I would have liked for her to go home. I would have liked her face small and pale behind the dirty windows of a Greyhound, the bus barreling toward Great Falls, coming out onto the wide plateau of the Rocky Mountain Front, then heading north toward Choteau and Heart Butte and Browning. I would have liked to see her step out into the great cradle of her own landscape. Home, she would have thought, this place I can claim and which claims me. The spine of the mountains rising to the west, silky and sensuous under deep snow. Eastward the slap of the wind across flat wheatlands and scrub.

I called Riley when I got home. It was late and his voice was groggy, but when I told him I needed to talk to him he said he'd be over right away. I hung up, laid Amos's tape on the kitchen table, and stared hard at it, as if the correct course of action might reveal itself to me.

I finished off one glass of bourbon and poured myself another. Riley lived up Grant Creek, and I knew it would be a good half hour before he got to my place. It was quiet in the house and I wanted Kristof to come, knew for certain he wouldn't.

Late last fall Kristof and I drove into Idaho to the hot springs, the ones off the Lochsa River, not far from where Bennett's plane went down. It was a beautiful day, Indian summer, the sky crisp and blue, incandescent. The woods reeked of warm pine sap. We hiked in several miles, the trail beneath our feet knobby with roots and half-buried stones. There were people down at the lower pools by the creek, loud hippies, naked and raucous. So we hiked farther in than usual and found a quiet pool up in the back of the drainage.

Autumn can be a tricky time of year in Montana. The days are still uncommonly long and the shift toward winter darkness is swift. Once night comes, it comes quickly. Maybe it was the warmth of the day that fooled us, or the steep cliffs that lined the drainage and obscured the sky, leaving only a narrow V of cloudless blue visible. Whatever the reason, we miscalculated the hours of sunlight left in the afternoon.

By the time we got dressed and started out, the woods were already smoky with shadows. I had to strain my eyes to see the blank ribbon of the trail. If you've ever been in it, you would know that darkness like that is a solid thing. Because you have a sense of what was once visible, you are not really blind, and your eyes become a handicap, a source of infinite deception.

We stumbled along, following the sound of the creek and the sharp line of the cliffs against the star-littered sky. At one point we plunged into the undergrowth and Kristof stopped short in front of me. I reached my hand out, feeling for him, for the soft nap of the green shirt. My palm found the scaly trunk of a ponderosa.

'Take your shoes off,' he said.

I let go of the tree and moved toward his voice. 'What?'

'Take your shoes off. Your socks too.'

I unlaced my boots and stepped out of them, peeling off my socks. The ground was soft and spongy, prickly with pine needles. We circled back in the direction we had come from, searching for the trail with the soles of our feet, stepping through tangles of thistles, soft beds of moss.

I would like to be able to say that once we found the cool pack of dirt with our toes that night I believed he would deliver us, unscathed. But the truth is that I was deathly afraid. And it was not him I mistrusted, but myself, my own failing senses. I thought we would lose each other, lose ourselves.

That was the difference between us: his faith and my lack of it. He never once doubted we would emerge and I never quite believed. Even when we crossed over the old rope bridge and saw a car pass on the narrow highway, its headlights sweeping across the canyon walls, lighting the rock, the trees, lighting the green eyes of animals – even then I chose faithlessness.

Headlights raked across the leafless skeleton of the maple tree in my front yard. I took my glass to the front window and peered out. A car looped around, pulled up behind my truck, and a man stepped onto the curb, his face backlit by the Christmas lights across the street. I watched him come forward, took in the machinery of bones and muscles, the delicacy of his body. For an instant, from the way he walked, the way he dipped his head, I was convinced it was Kristof.

How many times had I seen him in the dark? And still I fooled myself.

I moved closer to the window, watched the man take a step forward, his arms swinging at his sides. I closed my eyes and imagined the warm V of skin where his shirt opened.

Here's the ground, I thought, and here the cliff plunging toward the creek bed. Here are my own unreliable limbs beneath me, the darkness of my body, the blackness it contains. And out there the wild geography of uncertainty, the woods into which we must go, the disorder of it all, the trail that leads out. It's a simple choice, really, one direction over another.

The man stepped into the luminous arc of my porch light and his face leapt out, sharp and defined: Jeff Riley.

We sat at the table with Amos's tape between us. I poured Riley a drink, watched him gulp it appreciatively.

'Did I get you out of bed?' I asked.

He shook his head, but I knew he was lying. There was a deep crease in his cheek from the seam of a pillowcase. 'Been with the wife's family all day,' he said, setting the bourbon down. 'You have a good holiday?'

I shrugged, lit a cigarette.

He fidgeted, tapping the table with his thumb. 'So what's this about?'

I pushed the tape to his side of the table. 'I ran across this the other day. Thought you might be interested. It's funny the things you find in my business.'

Part of me knew it was a pointless gesture. Tina was dead, and so was Josie. The less I had to do with this whole mess, the better. But it was the only gesture I could make, and I felt I had to do something. Besides, there was still Tina's friend, Elton, to think about.

I offered Riley a cigarette and he took it, lit it greedily, and inhaled. 'Goddamn, that tastes good,' he said. 'You know, I never meant to accuse you, Meg. We had to cover all the bases is all. You should have told us you were with that foreign fellow. Turns out it was some gang out of California. You know, the drugs and all. At least that's what the father thinks. We're pretty sure he's right on the money.'

It was a strange conclusion, wishful thinking on Riley's part yet oddly predictable. It's not that people here are naïve. It's just that we would rather believe in the plague of outsiders. We'd rather keep our faith in our neighbors until the bitter end. Another Indian hit by a train, we like to say. Another killing up in Browning. One more narrow escape, a close call with the outside culture of violence that swoops down off the interstate and is gone again by morning.

An icicle dislodged itself from the eaves, fell past the kitchen window. 'It's warming up,' Riley commented. 'Feels like a chinook.' He grabbed the tape, stood as if to go. 'What's on here?' he asked.

I shrugged. 'You'll have to watch it for yourself.'

It was the sixth of January when I drove up to the High Line, twelve days after Christmas. The springlike winds of the chinook had come and gone like a benevolent army of invaders, and winter had returned. I had a possible repo to check on, a couple from Arizona who'd been hiding out and had recently surfaced outside of Babb. General Motors had been tracking them for a while, and it promised to be good money if I delivered.

I drove to the location I'd been given, a busted-up trailer in the woods outside of town, right up next to the Canadian border. The couple had cleared out already. They'd left the door ajar and wild animals had gotten inside and scavenged the place. The cupboards were thrown open and flour and sugar were strewn across the counters and floor. I figured a bear must have been involved because the refrigerator was knocked on its side. Smashed eggshells were licked clean. A pool of milk had frozen on the linoleum in front of the stove. It looked like maybe a big grizzly had come in and baked a birthday cake.

I hadn't intended to stop in Browning, but it was snowing hard when I got there and I was hungry and ready for a break. I stopped at a café in town and got a burger and a cup of coffee. It was a slow day, midafternoon. Aside from the waitress and the cook, I was the only person in the place. I watched cars glide by out the window and thought of my mother driving, the smell of stale cigarettes in our station wagon.

The waitress, a pretty Blackfeet woman, came with my check.

'Can I get you anything else?' she asked.

I shook my head. 'Should I pay you?'

The woman laughed. 'Don't see anyone else, do you?'

I handed her a ten-dollar bill. She reached into her apron and counted out my change.

'Did you grow up here?' I asked. She seemed so pleasant, so obliging.

'Yup.'

'Did you know the Red Deers?'

She looked up and scowled. I could see myself reflected in her silver belt buckle: white face, blue eyes, hair gathered back behind my head.

'A woman and her daughter,' I said, trying to sound friendly, an old acquaintance passing through. 'They lived outside of town. In a white house.' I smiled. 'The girl's about my age. My father used to work up here when I was a kid. We knew each other then.'

'You mean Henrietta Red Deer,' she said amiably. 'They live out Boarding School Road.' She looked at me knowingly, raised her hand, and pointed over my shoulder. 'That's north of town.'

'Thank you.' I smiled.

I can't tell you what I imagined, what I was thinking as I drove out through an ebbing squall. The land around Browning was as unfamiliar to me as a Georgia swamp might have been. No mountains here, just the Great Plains laid bare. The fields were white and exposed, dotted with wheat stubble and the occasional oil pump, one arm pounding the frozen ground relentlessly. I knew what little oil the wells actually yielded, and there was something plaintive about their constant hammering.

I had the best intentions. I guess I pictured redemption, my hand on Henrietta Red Deer's small back. It was a mistake, I would say. Your child, your Tina, was no killer. See, I have come with this news. I have not deserted you. I am not my father's daughter.

The road forked and I stuck to the right, to Boarding School Road. The trip was shorter than I'd remembered, time flattened out by age. To the east I could see the horizontal line of Rimrock Butte, to the west the bald black teeth of the mountains. There was just a hint of dusk in the sky, the clouds a shade darker than at midday, the snow catching the first glimmers of rose or blue or fiery orange. The house loomed out of the prairie like a ship locked in a frozen sea. A tangle of smoke wreathed up from the chimney, and the windows glowed with warm light.

I guess I imagined them grateful, beholden, even. I imagined my whole life, each second hammered out with one purpose in mind: to be this messenger.

I turned onto the driveway as my mother had turned onto it all those years ago. The house was tidy as I'd remembered. A pine wreath with a red bow hung from the front door. There was a kindling box on the porch, a few logs stacked neatly next to it. I pulled up behind a red Subaru, cut the engine, and got out. The porch light flipped on and a head appeared behind the lace curtains of the door. Out here you would know you had visitors before the doorbell even rang. You would hear each car that passed on the road.

I started up the steps and the door opened. A woman craned her head out, her smile huge, warm, her lips the color of fresh cranberries. She was striking, close to thirty, youthful, healthy, with hair dark as the tip of a magpie's wings. A baby sat on her hip.

'Can I help you?' she said cheerfully. Her skin was light, dotted with a few fading freckles. 'Maybe you're looking for the McCarthys? They're the next house down the road.'

'No,' I told her. 'I'm looking for Henrietta. Is she here?'

The baby smiled, beat his fists joyfully against her chest, wiggled his hips like he was riding a horse. She put her lips gently to the crown of his head.

'I'm Henrietta. Are you a parent?'

I looked at her blankly.

'A parent?' she repeated. 'Do I have one of your children in class this year?'

'No,' I told her.

She shifted the baby's weight and pushed the door open wider. 'Come in,' she said. 'I need to get this bread out of the oven.'

I followed her into the front hall and back to the kitchen. There was dough rising on the counter, fat round loaves under clean cotton dish towels. The entire house smelled of yeast and flour. It was a place I could have stayed forever, warm and tidy and completely void of chaos. Not a place where I belonged.

'I think I'm looking for your mother,' I said, as the woman opened the oven and pulled out a perfect loaf with her one babyless hand.

'I thought you said you were looking for Henrietta.' She put the bread on the counter. 'My mother's name is Nola.'

'Is she here?'

The woman was becoming wary, and I started to think I had made a huge mistake.

'I'm sorry,' I told her, smiling. 'I'm confused. I was here as a child.'

'It's okay,' she said, trying to be kind. 'My mother does live here. With me and my husband. She's at work now, though.'

'What does she do?' I asked.

The woman looked at me skeptically. 'She's a lawyer for the tribe.'

'Oh.' I shuffled my feet awkwardly, looked down at the clean wood floor. 'I should go.'

She walked me to the door, relief written large on her face. No, I did not belong here. My clothes were sour, stained with coffee and salt. I could smell the cigarette smoke in my hair, yesterday's liquor in my sweat. I had nothing to give this woman, and for once I knew it.

'Can I take a message for my mother?' she asked.

I shook my head, started down the steps, then turned back. 'Do you have a sister?' I asked. 'Tina Red Deer?'

The baby giggled, pursed its tiny lips, and blew spit bubbles.

Henrietta looked at me. Her nose was slightly crooked, humped at the bridge. Like my father's nose, and mine.

'No,' she said. 'It's just me. But there are lots of Red Deers up here, you know.'

I could see her in my rearview mirror as I drove away. My sister stood in the doorway and watched me go. Only when I reached the end of the driveway did her head disappear. There was a car coming toward me along Boarding School Road, a sporty little Saab with its running lights on. I sat in the driveway and waited for it to pass, but it slowed and hit its blinker. I pulled out to let the Saab in and for a moment I was just a foot or two away from the driver.

It was another woman, an older, slightly darker

copy of the one with the baby. Her hair was pulled back in a graceful bun. She wore a traditional necklace, bright bones against her dark shirt. She was elegant and smart. She looked at me as we passed, smiled graciously. Another one lost, she might have thought. Or another one selling something: religion, cleaning supplies, things she didn't need. Or she might not have given me any thought at all.